Nancy can never forget...

"Nancy. Leila. Wake up!" A strong hand rudely shook her.

"Mama?" Nancy rubbed her eyes. "I can't see you." She took in a deep breath. "Why is it so hard to breathe?" She coughed and her eyes smarted. "Mama, why—?"

"Run outside, Nancy. Now!" Her mother snatched her from the bed she and Leila shared. "Don't stop for anything, no matter what happens. Get outside, you hear me?"...

Nancy screamed. Fire leaped between them, a wall of flame so hot the child shrank back. "Mama, where are you?" she wailed.

"Run, Nancy!" The hoarse command rang in the five-year-old's ears, along with Leila's frightened cries. In the heartbeat before Nancy fled, the curtain of flames lifted just enough for a final glimpse of her mother's agonized face, Leila's outstretched arms. Then with a demonic shriek, the fire roared hotter and higher. Nancy stumbled backwards.

"Run, darling. Mama loves you!"...

A loud shout, strong arms, a voice saying, "It's all right, child; we'll get you out."

Nancy struggled to a sitting position, in shock until some of her pain subsided... A dark figure dashed across her field of vision.

For a single moment she saw his face, etched against the lurid light of flickering flames.

She never forgot. . . .

CONNIE LORAINE is the pen name of a well-established novelist who always wanted to write and always wanted to be a nurse. Despite her choice of career, her lifelong interest in nursing is put to good use when she writes, as she does frequently, about nurses, doctors, and hospitals.

Books by Connie Loraine

HEARTSONG PRESENTS
HP85—Lamp in Darkness

Flickering
Flames

Connie Loraine

Shepherd of Love Hospital Series: Book Two

Heartsong Presents

ISBN 1-55748-698-0
FLICKERING FLAMES

PRINTED IN THE U.S.A.

prologue

For a single moment, she saw his face—etched against the lurid light of flickering flames.

She never forgot.

Twenty years later, she saw his face again—outlined against a sun-glorified stained-glass window.

She never forgot.

one

*Thy word is a lamp unto my feet,
and a light unto my path.* (Psalm 119:105)

Nancy Galbraith, R.N., never passed the director's office at Seattle's Shepherd of Love Hospital without stopping to read the inscription neatly engraved on the door. Tall, dark-skinned, with warm dark eyes that glowed with love for her job and her Lord, she also always breathed a prayer of gratitude. Today, she glanced both ways, then ran a slim brown finger over the words. "This old world needs all the light you have to offer, Lord," she whispered. "Please, help me be able to give to others, as You have given to me."

The prayer steadied her. She smoothed her soft peach pantsuit over her waist and hips, drew herself to her full five feet, eight inches height and smiled. Even after her years at the hospital conceived in response to God's leading,* Nancy retained some of the training-school fear that always accompanied a summons to the director's office.

She raised one silky eyebrow and murmured, "A psychiatrist could have a field day with you," then determinedly shoved back unwelcome thoughts and tapped lightly on the open door. She received no answer, so she stepped inside. Her fetish for promptness exacted a price.

Shepherd of Love Hospital Series: Book One—Lamp in Darkness

Always early, she spent time waiting for others. Ten minutes remained before her scheduled appointment.

"I hope it doesn't take long," she fretted and stretched her 140-pound, streamlined body. Not an ounce of fat marred her strong muscles and graceful curves. The unstinting care and ministry she gave her small patients in the Pediatrics Department kept her trim. So did the mile-or-more daily walks she took regularly.

Nancy wandered to the window that overlooked Puget Sound, white-capped with March waves and sparkling in the early spring sunlight. How simple and in keeping with the mood was the hospital director's office. Paneled walls and muted carpeting plus a serviceable desk and comfortable chairs provided a restful atmosphere with no trace of ostentation. Just like the hospital itself, Nancy thought, with its white stone walls warmed to cream by the sun. She loved every inch of the sprawling two-story complex on the wooded slope above the Sound. It had become home when she had despaired of ever having a home again. Bible verses and land, sea, and mountain murals graced the walls, quiet reminders to patients, staff, and visitors of God's love and creation.

"How nice you look, Nancy." The hospital director came to stand beside her. Keen-eyed, modestly dressed, he kept his capable fingers on the pulse of the hospital without undue interference. His rare ability to make employees feel they worked *with* him, not *for* him, contributed much to the close bonds that inspired each individual to give excellent service.

"The children especially love the colored uniforms."

She smiled at him. "And I'm glad we allow each nurse to choose the colors she likes best."

His eyes twinkled. "A suggestion of yours, if I remember correctly."

"Self-defense," she teased. Her eyes shone with fun. "Peach, pink, and yellow are my colors. If I had to wear lavender or green I'm not sure I could do my work well. They make my skin look muddy." He laughed appreciatively and she added, "I'm sure you didn't call me in to discuss uniforms, right?"

"Right." He motioned her to a chair and dropped into the swiveled one behind his desk. "I've—oh, here he is now. Dr. Barton, come in."

Nancy's usually reliable heart skipped a beat. In the time it took for the hospital director to shake hands with the white-coated newcomer, she surveyed Dr. Barton— and found him pleasing. Six feet tall, probably 180 pounds, short black hair, springy but not kinky, skin a shade darker than her own and a white smile that relieved the look of sadness his face held when in repose. She knew he was 33 and the quickly-veiled look in his beautiful black eyes did nothing toward steadying her heartbeat.

I wonder why he isn't married. Or is he? Nancy glanced down at her capable hands and willed the hot color she felt warm her face to recede.

The director's voice snapped her to professionalism. "I asked Dr. Barton to meet with us, along with Dr. and Mrs. Paul Hamilton," he explained.

Who? It took Nancy a moment to make the connection. Such a short time had passed since Jonica Carr, R.N., Night Surgical Charge Nurse and Nancy's good friend, had become Mrs. Paul Hamilton that the hospital hadn't yet grown used to her new name. It actually didn't matter much; the staff's first-name basis added warmth to their association. Nancy remembered their simple but beautiful wedding in the hospital chapel, the pledges and lighted candle that signified both love and service to one another, God, and His children. Her eyes stung. Would she one day stand making such vows by candlelight? Or would the memory of flickering flames continue to burn hot and fierce, erupting into nightmares that awakened her with their intensity?

It took all her poise and self control to slam shut the door of her past and greet the tall, brown-haired, blue-eyed Jonica and her dark-haired, dark-eyed surgeon husband when they entered. Minutes later, the hospital director turned to Dr. Paul. "It's all yours."

Dr. Paul's face shone with excitement. "Jonica and I have an announcement." The words tumbled out in his eagerness to share. "We've been talking with Dad, Nicholas Fairchild, and a few others and have decided we need to add to the downtown Shepherd of Love Sanctuary. The clinic is good; so is our shelter. Yet it isn't enough. What we need is a better program for the children, especially those under five. Single mothers are caught in the crunch of not being able to afford decent child care on their welfare checks, which means they can't work and get off welfare." His eyes flashed. "I know there are all kinds of so-called 'care centers'. Some are good. A lot aren't. What we visualize is a service that will include Bible teaching. Any parent who wants to enroll a child in the Shepherd of Love Care Center will agree to allow that child to be taught the truth of the gospel. In return, the Center will subsidize to whatever extent is needed."

"Won't a lot of people take advantage of free care?" Dr. Barton looked doubtful.

"It won't be free, Damon," Dr. Paul leaned forward. "We plan to offer counseling and will sit down with each parent and work out what they can reasonably afford. Otherwise, we'd be subject to misuse. This way, people who are willing to work can feel pride in knowing they're doing their best."

"Where do we come in?" Nancy inquired.

"Along with the care center, we want to do a children's clinic once a week. We're hoping we can get some help from the regular hospital personnel, plus those who come in on a consultant basis such as you, Damon."

Dr. Barton groaned. "Give me an eighth day every week and I'll be happy to oblige." He drew his brows together and looked troubled. "I already owe so much to Dr. Cranston for taking me into his private practice, I don't know how much more time I can honestly be away from it. He's been wonderful about the consulting I do for Shepherd of Love, but. . ." His voice trailed off.

Nancy understood his dilemma. Hospital personnel affectionately discussed one another and talk had it that Damon deserved everything he had in the way of prestige. She also caught his regret.

"We understand." Jonica's eyes looked like twin sapphires. "Once we get totally established, Nicholas says we'll hire more staff. We're not asking you to commit each week, Dr. Barton. Paul and I plan to screen. What we need from you is the knowledge we can refer specialty cases to you, many from those who won't be able to pay."

Relief brightened Damon's face. "I can promise you that," he quietly told them. "There's no reason such appointments can't be scheduled in my free time, is there?"

"Free time!" Nancy burst out, then bit her lip. No one knew better than she how much time the dedicated children's specialist spent in simply visiting Pediatrics and chatting with the small patients.

His eyes twinkled, although he solemnly said, "Really, Nurse Galbraith. I almost always am free between two and four a.m. Of course,..." He stroked his smooth-shaven chin reflectively. "That might not be the most convenient time for the patients."

The room exploded in laughter and Nancy found herself caught up in it. A flood of joy that God had led her faltering steps to Shepherd of Love and co-workers such as these brought a bright mist to her long lashes and she quickly blinked it away.

"Nancy, what about you? Swamped, as usual?" Jonica asked.

"And how!" She spread her hands out in mock despair. "I sometimes think that every time I get a nurse trained the way I want her she immediately decides this is the time for her to marry. We've lost three in the last year." She grimaced. "I'm considering renaming Pediatrics Galbraith Matrimonial."

"Hmmm. Might not be a bad idea." Dr. Barton's grin did strange things to Nancy. *What did he mean by that, anyway?* She didn't dare ask. Instead she sighed.

"Give me a few weeks to straighten out the schedule and I can probably work it so I can help at least sometimes." A thought gripped her. "I have an idea. Why not send advanced students from the training schools who do affiliation here down in relays as part of their training? They'll get a whole different perspective than what we offer here."

"Great!" Dr. Paul clasped his hands above his head in a prize-fight winning gesture. "By their final year, students will be more than able to handle most of the patients. Then if Jonica or one other registered nurse plus myself—Dad and Emily can help, too—are around, we're set." The informal meeting ended on a high note of hope, with joined hands and a prayer for guidance from their Chief, whose children they longed to serve.

Dr. Paul and Jonica vanished down the hall. The director ruefully confessed he had a "million, more or less" reports. Dr. Barton followed Nancy toward the stairs that led to the second story and Pediatrics.

"Nancy, are you losing weight?"

Astonishment stopped her in her tracks. "Why, no. Why do you ask?"

His searching gaze never left her face. "Your eyes are shadowed except when you laugh." Genuine concern underscored every word. "Is something bothering you?"

An unfamiliar warmth crept into her heart. Few of her associates, even Jonica or the other nurses, Patty, Lindsey, and Shina, saw beneath the cool mask she wore except when working with the children. To her horror, a large, hot drop fell and splashed on her hand. The price she paid for keeping an emotional distance from others also brought loneliness.

Damon's frank questions chipped away at her reserve. She looked down, hoping he hadn't noticed, but the action was in vain. The same trained eyes that never missed a child's woe could scarcely overlook Nancy's temporary letdown.

"Come." A strong hand guided her away from the staircase and across the large, skylighted Central Waiting area. They paused just inside the chapel door. "Good. It's empty." Dr. Barton seated her and dropped down beside her. "All right. What's the matter?"

If only she could tell him. If only she could put her head on his broad shoulder and spill out everything swarming in her mind and heart like angry bees. Instead, she shook her head.

"I've known for weeks something inside is keeping you upset," he quietly told her. He made no effort to touch her but went on talking in his mellow voice. "It hasn't affected your work, yet. . ."

What he left unsaid struck her harder than a blow. "It mustn't," she whispered. "The children. They're my life."

She felt her lips tremble and pressed them together hard to steady herself. She heard the swift intake of breath before he said, "You're personally involved."

"Yes." The thing she had feared and dreaded came into the open. The single affirmative expressed her deepest doubts. She felt she must make him understand. "I know a nurse isn't supposed to take patients into her heart. I had it drummed into me all during training. *Be compassionate but dispassionate* is the motto. I've tried, Damon."

"And now?" He still didn't touch her but she noticed how tightly his hands lay clenched on his knee.

"I just don't know." The words dragged out, dreary, foreboding. "During the past months I haven't been able to leave the children on the ward. They perch on my shoulder, sit on my bed, crying and pleading for my help with outstretched arms." The dam inside sprang a leak and a few more hot tears escaped. They didn't seem to matter. Nancy went on, "I'm so drained. I pray for strength and it comes, but just enough to complete my shift. I can't give up my work but I can't go on like this, either."

"Are you sleeping?"

"Not very well," she confessed and wiped away the tears with a tissue from her pocket.

"Nightmares?"

"Yes."

"What about?"

She couldn't tell him. Only to God could she open up the past. She hedged. "Distorted images. Frightening things. Death and fire." She clamped her lips shut. Beyond that she would not, could not go, even to the doctor who had in the last few minutes become a person she instinctively felt she could trust with anything—except her secret.

He rested his hand on hers and his rich voice deepened. "Nancy, if you had a broken leg, would you trust me when I told you it had to be set?"

Odd that he would ask her that just when she had been thinking of trust. She mutely nodded, glad for the warm pressure of his hand.

"I am not a professional counselor but I believe from what I see as changes in you and what you've said that you need to talk with someone who is."

She felt sick. Why had she confessed her problem? He wanted her to see a shrink. Did he think she was tottering on the edge of a nervous breakdown? The thought chilled her. She started to stand, to free her hand. He tightened his hold and firmly restrained her. She refused to struggle but froze when he told her, "Why is it that even medical personnel refuse to recognize the validity of emotional trauma when it comes to their own lives? Nancy Galbraith, you can't keep on the way you're going."

Rage flamed. She snatched her hand away and leaped to her feet. "You think I'm crazy! I was a fool to believe you." She bit back accusations, ran toward the other open end of the pew and freedom.

He caught her at the chapel door. Sadness gleamed in his black eyes when he looked down at her. "I don't think that at all. I just know you need help." His face turned to granite. "I've been there. I reacted the same way you did, except for a different reason. Only the grace of God saved me, Nancy."

Too filled with pain and mortification plus an appalling sense of loss, she refused to listen to either his unspoken or spoken message. "I have to get back to work, Dr. Barton."

He silently stepped aside and let her go. She proudly raised her head and marched away, stony-faced, mask once more in place. Yet her traitorous heart longed to stay. . . .

Nancy worked on long beyond her shift, reading to the children, overseeing her staff, anything to delay going to her suite in the staff residence building. She got by with skipping dinner without anyone noticing. Tonight the soft green walls of the staff dining room would be prison walls.

Besides, for all she knew Dr. Damon Barton might show up unexpectedly and she needed time. She thought of a tune from the musical *Camelot* in which the heroine realizes that before she sees the one she loves again there must be a time to weep, to forget.

Her lovely lips twisted. Guenevere and Lancelot's troubles were a myth; hers were real, raw, demanding. She reluctantly left Pediatrics, slowly walked down the curving staircase to Central Waiting, then made her way across to the long, covered walk to the place she called home, praying she wouldn't run into her friends. Blond Patty from Outpatient; freckled, red-headed efficient Lindsey from Surgery; tiny Japanese Shina from Obstetrics all roomed at the far end of the first floor suites past the community living room, library, game room, and laundry. Any of them would be happy to talk with her, yet their more carefree upbringings made them seem years younger at twenty-three than Nancy at twenty-five. She toyed with the idea of calling Jonica, then shook her head. Her friend had also suffered an unpleasant childhood but Dr. Paul's love had gradually brought her away from bad memories. Why inflict more on the woman as sensitive as Nancy herself?

She concentrated on good things: the way Jonica's mother had miraculously recuperated from malnutrition and open heart surgery; how even now she was nearly ready to graduate from intermediate care to a place in Dr. Paul's father's home as housekeeper while Dr. Peter and his wife of a few months, Emily, continued their medical careers.

Nancy heaved a sigh of relief when she fled through the deserted living room and hall and reached the haven of her rose and white suite. A quick shower and a hasty soup-and-salad supper raised her spirits enough so she could evaluate the confrontation with Dr. Barton more objectively. Using a trick learned from Nicholas Fairchild, founder of Shepherd of Love, she spread the scene in her mind and replayed it with the roles reversed. Nicholas, who always found time to talk with anyone at the hospital available, had said, "It helps to pretend I'm the other person. I get a whole new look at things."

Now Nancy said aloud, "If I had been the doctor and he had told me what I told him would I have reacted the same way?" The total honesty that characterized her brought a quiet, "Yes."

"God, do I really need counseling? I thought I'd overcome all that garbage and tragedy." The low prayer only
made her face the issue. "Is it really that I'm taking the
children's problems too much to heart, or does it go a lot
deeper? Do I need to face things again?" She felt her
insides recoil at the thought. "Forgive me for anger and
give me the courage to become whole."

Nancy gasped at the prayer. Never had she prayed in
exactly that way. Had the Holy Spirit Who guides into
truth led her faltering tongue? She mulled it over while
straightening up an already-immaculate room and
laying out a soft yellow pantsuit uniform for the next
morning. Heart pounding, she went into her tastefully
decorated bedroom, thankful she roomed alone. She followed her nightly routine. A good face wash. Cream on
her hands. A fluffy pink gown.

Yet tonight she varied. Instead of slipping into the
nightgown, she took off the sports blouse she'd donned
after her shower and deliberately turned her back to the
large dresser mirror. For the first time in years she looked
over her shoulder, braced herself, and swallowed hard.
Faint scars crisscrossed the otherwise brown-velvet skin.
Plastic surgery had done wonders but had failed to con-
ceal the final evidence. Her practiced gaze noticed how
much the scars had faded but sweat popped out on her
body from the memories they evoked. It took a second
shower and a glass of warm milk to settle her down
enough to sleep, and when she did, flames flickered
around her and childish voices called.

two

"Nurse Nancy." Five-year-old Timmy clutched at her arm. "I'm thirsty." Feverish and bright-eyed, he lay spreadeagled in bed clothes tangled with his tossing.

"Good for you!" Nancy smiled, reached for his drinking glass with the bent straw, and handed it to him. "The more you drink, the quicker your temperature will go down."

"Then bring me the ocean, please." Timmy noisily gurgled down water through the straw.

Several children looked their way when their nurse laughed. Shepherd of Love preferred housing their young patients several to a room and reserved the semi-privates and a very few private rooms for those with contagious diseases or children needing special care.

"If you drank ocean water, you would really be thirsty," Nancy told her small friend. "You know how badly you want a drink after you eat salty popcorn and things like that? Well, the ocean is a lot saltier. Besides, the only way anyone can drink ocean water is if it goes through a process to remove the salt." She never talked down to those she served. Her healthy respect for children required endless explanations and answers to dozens of questions each shift. A typical workday could include,

19

"Are there polar bears in heaven," "Do grasshoppers sleep," "Will Daddy come back to Mommy and me," "Is God as big as the Seattle Center," and "Do you have a little boy like me?"

Nancy conscientiously answered as best she could and when she had no answer she frankly admitted, "I don't know but I'll look it up for you." At other time she simply held a little hand and quietly said, "No one knows that, dear, but God. We can trust Him." If deep inside she winced at the memory of a time she had trusted God and He hadn't done what she asked, only her understanding Creator knew.

Now Timmy heaved a sigh of relief when her capable hands smoothed crumpled sheets, plumped his pillow, and bathed his hot face with cool water. "Nurse Nancy, when I go home, will you go with me?"

Her hands stilled. *Please, God, tell me what to say.* She waited, forced a smile. Timmy would be going home soon but not to his family. He was one of the chief reasons she had gone so far as to consider giving up Pediatric nursing. His wasted body grew more frail every day and all the staff could do was watch and give loving care to make him comfortable. Consultations with Dr. Barton and the mother had resulted in the decision to leave him in his familiar surroundings as long as possible.

"Will you? Please?"

Nancy marveled at the steadiness of her voice when she told him, "Timmy, you won't need me. You're going to be well. Although I'd love to be with you, what about all your friends here—the children who are still sick?"

Understanding crept into his intelligent face. It fought with his own needs. "Won't you ever come?"

"Someday," she said through stiff lips. To hide her emotion she bent over, carefully hugged him, then made a big show of fluffing his pillow again. "Enough questions, young man." She shook her finger at him. "It's time you took a nap. The same goes for you and you and you," she sternly told the others, who giggled into their pillows, even while settling down. Experience had taught that Nurse Nancy meant what she said but the twinkle in her dark eyes showed how much she cared about them.

"Nurse Nancy, will you sing? It's easier to go to sleep." Timmy peered up at her, face a little less flushed. "Then when I wake up, Mother will be here."

The poignancy in the way he said Mother touched his nurse's heart. For the hundredth time she longed for a day when she would have children of her own and not just be a substitute mother to those who came, claimed part of her heart, and went away to forget her when released. Or those like Timmy, who carried part of her with them when God called. "Let's all sing a song together," she suggested. She patted Timmy's hand, made her rounds to check and hug each of her small patients and began the song in her untrained but beautiful voice.

> *Jesus loves the little children*
> *All the children of the world;*
> *Red and yellow, black and white,*
> *They are precious in His sight.*

Jesus loves the little children of the world.

Nancy thought as she sang, accompanied by her charges' clear, treble voices, *the anonymous author could well have stood in my shoes and written these words.* Her loving gaze rested on Vietnamese, Black, Mexican-American, and various shades of white-to-tan faces; innocent faces, precious in the sight of the Lord. Knowledge swelled within her. She belonged here. No matter how hard, how pulled she felt, her ministry lay in exactly what she now gave. God would grant her strength to endure, for the sake of these children—and Leila.

Helped by long practice, she jerked her attention back to the ward and away from deeply buried events that persisted in returning to haunt her. The song ended. The children obediently closed their eyes, even though, "We're not sleepy," Timmy loftily informed her.

"You don't have to sleep if you don't want to," she told him. "Just rest your eyes."

"Aw, that's what you said before, and the next thing I knew I woke up and Mother was here." Timmy eyed her distrustfully then stretched his mouth in a wide, gap-toothed smile.

It nearly proved to be her undoing. She managed an answering smile and figuratively bolted, although her smooth, graceful walk remained slow, as usual. Blinded by her fight to retain control, she walked toward the desk that served as a hub for surrounding rooms, staring at the floor. Her first awareness of another's presence came in the form of two highly polished black shoes just in front of her.

Nancy looked up. Gasped. "Dr. Barton. I didn't hear you come in." Why, oh why, had he caught her just now? All her hastily assembled poise wouldn't fool him. She read in his black eyes the same concern that had been there the previous day and dreaded what lay ahead.

Damon started to speak then stopped. She relaxed tense muscles when he grinned companionably and confessed, "I just wish I'd been here a few minutes sooner. I have a not-so-terrible bass voice and love to sing. Although you and the children certainly didn't appear to need my help."

She caught her breath and smiled at him, thankful for his teasing. "They really do fall asleep better if we sing."

"Sometimes I've heard you singing to them," he huskily said. The planes of his face softened and some of his perennial sadness fled for a moment. "It reminded me of my mother singing to my br—to me when I was a child. You are very like her, Nancy."

She could feel her pulse quicken. "Thank you." Without considering the consequences she added, "I sang to Leila."

His silent questioning glance brought realization of the door she'd opened and she hastily added, "My sister. She died, a long time ago." Tears clogged her throat.

"I'm sorry."

His genuine compassion unnerved her. "It happened twenty years ago. You'd think after all this time. . ." The rest of her explanation wouldn't come. She wordlessly thanked God when the telephone rang, and while she dealt with the caller, Damon lifted a hand in farewell and walked away. The rest of the day, with the admission of two new patients, kept Nancy so busy she had little time for either remembering or soul-searching, and her contact with Dr. Barton over the next few days related strictly to duty.

More than a week passed before she had time to speak with him seriously and it concerned Timmy. The little boy daily grew whiter and thinner. Most of the time he felt too tired to even laugh. As he failed, he clung even more closely to his beloved Nurse Nancy. One night long after her shift had ended, she returned to check on him, prompted by an inner sense that he needed her.

Timmy lay perfectly still but slow tears leaked from his wide-open eyes.

"Timmy, dearest, what is it?" Nancy knelt by his bedside and gathered his thin body in her strong arms, passionately wishing she could lend him the strength he needed.

"I-I don't want to be here," he whispered.

She sensed his carefulness not to disturb his sleeping friends. "Why not, Timmy?"

"They all—look at me." He huddled in her arms, a broken bird who soon would soar beyond his earthly troubles.

"Would you like to be in a private room?" she asked.

"If you're with me. Or Mother."

It cut to her heart, but why not? He couldn't last long, and it was better for him to request a transfer than being arbitrarily moved. "I'll talk with Dr. Barton tomorrow and see what we can do. Okay? Until then, your night nurse will take care of you." She stood long enough to reach for his chart on the end of the bed and note Timmy had been given a sedative a short while before. Good. It would take effect and release him from his childish woes.

"I-drather-have-you," he slurred. Moments later his even breathing told her the medication had done its work well. She held him a few minutes longer, then gently arranged his body in a more comfortable position. When she looked up, Damon stood on the other side of the bed. She didn't even question why. It felt right for him to be there.

They silently went out and as on the day of their confrontation, Damon led the way to the chapel, softly lighted and welcoming. Seated, she looked up at him. "You heard?"

"Enough to know what we have to do. Nancy, if you can handle it, I want you to special Timmy in a private room; to be there any time his mother can't. It's going to take a whole lot of emotional stamina and the ability to be objective. Can you do it?"

She longed to shout yes, to firmly convince him. Instead she stared at her hands. "I don't know." Something tore inside of her. "Why? Why does a loving God allow a child to die? What's the use of it? Why was Timmy, and others, ever born if they're to be struck down while young?" All the secret resentment she'd struggled with for years came to a boil and erupted. "Why, Damon? If God is love and we know He is, how can He. . ." A sob interrupted her questions.

"Nancy, my dar—" He broke off and took her hands in his. She felt his strength and rock-solid faith flow into her aching heart.

"I just want Timmy to be healed," she brokenly told him.

"He will be. Soon. Is it any less a miracle that Timmy, and others, are healed through death rather than in life?"

"What are you saying?" She stared at him in disbelief.

"Every Christian, every follower should know that death is the ultimate healing," Damon said in his resonant voice. "We doctors and nurses and surgeons and specialists do what I like to consider as temporary patch-up jobs. Through medicine and surgery, we repair bodies and minds. God, through death, restores those bodies and minds into eternal perfection. Nancy, would you have Timmy go on as he is, impaired, weak?"

"No, but God could heal him. We've seen many cases where He has," she quickly responded.

"But not all. Jesus didn't heal every leper, every blind person, every paralyzed individual, *in this life*. His mission included physical healing, but primarily, He came to give His own life to ensure eternal healing, of the soul as well as the body and mind. When He said He came that people might have life and that more abundantly* He didn't put a timeline on it. We live in an imperfect world and are subject to what happens. Sometimes, God in His wisdom, alters the natural course of events, but it doesn't lessen His majesty when He does not."

*John 10:10

"I recognize that. It's just so hard to see children who will never grow up and see the beauty God has given to us."

Damon increased the pressure of his hands on hers. "Nancy, the most gorgeous thing on earth is nothing compared with what Timmy is going to see when he enters the presence of God."

She felt some of her turmoil drain at the picture Damon had painted in such a few well-chosen words.

"I want to ask you again. Can you give Timmy the kind of send-off he needs? It won't be any more than a week, probably less."

She closed her eyes to shut out his face. Timmy's rose in its place, pleading for her love, skill, and comfort. His murmured, "I-drather-have-you" could not be denied. Nancy opened her wet eyes. "With the help of God, I can. The scripture is filled with promises that when our strength fails, He will supply. When shall I start?"

"Not tonight; Timmy will sleep. We'll talk with his mother tomorrow and arrange things. Instead of a private room, we'll use a semi-private so if she wants to stay nights, she can." He released her hands, stood, and looked down at her. "You are quite a woman, Nurse Nancy." He turned and walked out without looking back.

She stayed in the deserted chapel for a long time, wondering if Damon's voice had broken on his parting words. She told herself his partially completed word could not have been darling. In all the time they'd known one another, there had never been any spark between them except for their mutual dedication to their work.

Until now.

She shied at the thought that perched on her shoulder all the way to her suite. Sleep mercifully settled the question of further consideration, brought on by the exhaustion created by Timmy's need. Nine hours later she awakened to a sunny day, inner renewal, and the realization of how much her attitude had changed because of Damon sharing his faith and beliefs. If she could cling to what he had said the way Timmy clung to her, it could make all the difference.

Nancy's new assignment tested her mettle to the utmost. At Dr. Damon's insistence, Timmy was told how seriously ill he was. Nancy would never forget how the child's mother nodded then asked, "Would you tell him, Doctor?"

Damon hadn't hesitated. "Yes, but I want both of you there." Later that day, the three who loved Timmy so much had gathered around his bed.

"Hi." The little-boy grin looked too big for the white face. "All my fav'rit people, huh." He yawned and covered his mouth with a fist. "How come I'm so tired?" He yawned again. "Wish I could go to sleep and when I wake up, be all well."

Nancy truly believed the opening was an answer to all their prayers. She had agonized over it, so when Dr. Barton picked up on Timmy's wish and said, "Guess what, buddy. That's just what's going to happen," she shot an unspoken prayer of thanks toward heaven.

"Really?" His eyes brightened.

"Really, Timmy. You're going to be able to run and play and holler like you used to. Just one thing. Your mother and Nurse Nancy and I don't get to be with you for a while."

Fear flared in the bright eyes. "How come?"

Damon cocked his head to one side and his face glowed. "Remember when you played games and got to be first? How you'd run ahead of everyone and maybe hide around a bend of the trail and wait for your friends?"

"I remember." The fear faded. "I ran fast and got there before anyone else."

"Timmy, this time is kind of like that. You know someday we're all going to live in heaven with Jesus, don't you?"

"Yeah. Mother and me and you and Nurse Nancy and everybody who loves Him. Mother said so." A look of perfect trust shot from his eyes. The next minute he struggled into a sitting position. "You mean I'm going to heaven pretty soon?"

"Right, buddy."

Timmy thought it over. "And you'll come and find me, Mother? Like you used to come when I hid?"

"Pretty soon, son."

"Will you miss me 'til you get there?" he wanted to know.

"Very much." She blinked and Nancy wondered at her courage.

"And I won't be sick ever again?"

"Never!" Nancy found her voice, although she had felt not one word would come out. "You'll be strong and oh, Timmy, best of all, you'll get to see Jesus, before any of us." She took his hand. "When you get there, would you do something for me?"

"'Course." His face lit with the chance to please his beloved Nurse Nancy.

"My little sister Leila died when she was just your age. When you see her, and I'm sure you will, tell her I'll be coming soon." She hesitated. "Or maybe even before then, Jesus will come back to earth like He promised, and bring you and Leila with Him."

"Wow! That's neat." A spurt of energy sent a faint color into the thin cheeks. "Mother, you'll watch real good so you won't miss us, right?"

"Right," she promised.

He sank back on the pillow. "I wish all of us could go together, but if Jesus is there, I guess it'll be okay 'til you come." He fell silent and a speculative look crept into his eyes. "Nurse Nancy, sing that song. The one about the charyut coming. Maybe God'll send a charyut for me." His eyes closed with weakness.

How could she sing around the lump in her throat? How could she not sing? Gratitude poured through her when Damon began the time-honored words of the beloved Negro spiritual in his rich voice.

> *Swing low, sweet chariot,*
> *Comin' for to carry me home. . .*

A few lines later, Nancy joined in. Then Timmy's mother added a soft alto. Damon switched to bass and their voices blended into beauty.

> *I looked over Jordan and what did I see*
> *Comin' for to carry me home,*
> *A band of angels, comin' after me. . .*

Timmy's eyes opened. An indescribable look lit his face. He stretched out his arms, but not to the singers. The next moment his eyes closed. He sighed softly and Nancy knew his spirit had gone. The sadness she had expected didn't come. Was it the far-seeing look in the child's eyes at the last? Had he been granted a vision to comfort him in the twinkling between life and life eternal? She didn't know. She only knew that of all the people she had seen die during her years of nursing, never had she witnessed the kind of glory that still hovered in the quiet room.

Timmy's mother gathered her son into her lap and sat crooning. Yet the same wonder in Nancy's heart reflected in her tear-dimmed eyes when she looked up and told them, "I can never thank either of you enough."

Damon's comforting hand dropped to her shoulder. "Don't thank us, but the Holy Spirit. The presence of God attended Timmy's passing. Now, we'll leave you with him as long as you want to stay. Just come to the desk when you're ready to go."

Ten minutes later, she came out of Timmy's room and closed the door behind her. Much of the spirit experienced still surrounded her like an aura. In the time it took to get necessary information, she continued to hold up well, perhaps too well. Damon stayed while Nancy took down answers, but when the woman stood, he counseled her, "Right now what we shared is holding you up. It will continue to do so but only to a point. Do you have someone who can walk you through the grieving process in the next few months? No matter how strong our faith in God is, we still have to get beyond all the human emotions and find peace."

"The pastor of my church is also a trained counselor. He and his wife have already asked me to stay with them for a time," she responded. "I also have a widowed lady who will come be with me if I choose to remain at home." She paused. "And I know I can call on you."

"Day or night," Nancy promised and Damon nodded in agreement. After she left, Nancy spontaneously turned to him. "I wish I'd had someone like you, all those years ago."

His quiet answer revealed how deeply he had been moved by their shared experience. Deep lines etched into his face. "I do, too, Nancy." As if not trusting himself to say more, he turned and walked away, leaving her warmed, not only by his look of compassion but by the Spirit he carried in a heart made large through service and his abiding love for his Heavenly Father.

three

If only I could live on the mountaintops where I felt close to God all the time, how happy I'd be. Nancy shrugged off the thought. She'd once heard a minister say, "For every mountain, there's a valley." How true. And how easy to slide back into the valley of despondency after even the highest, most poignant experience. She had hoped Timmy's death would strengthen her. It had, until she went back on duty and saw his empty bed. She felt herself crumple inside. Doubts dimmed the memory of his passing and attacked with renewed vigor. Days fled into weeks and spring limped into early summer. Still the troubled nurse kept her own counsel, refusing to admit she couldn't handle her life the way she must in order to continue in Pediatrics.

Nancy knew Dr. Barton observed her struggles but steeled herself against his unspoken invitation to unburden herself.

"When I can get past losing Timmy, I'll think about other things," she promised herself. Yet more and more she allowed the thought of seeking professional counseling to seep into her reluctant heart.

She had gone to see Timmy's mother a few days after the memorial service, which she had also attended, being glad it stressed life rather than death. For the first time in her nursing career, she felt uncertain. How did one approach a grieving mother who shed tears yet wore the same radiance her son had donned in his hospital bed?

"I am so glad you came." Warm, welcoming hands drew her into the house and into a circle of love. "Would you like to see Timmy's room?" She led the way to a typical little-boy's room; airplanes strewn on the wallpaper; a matching bedspread, far smoother than when it had covered a small frame.

Nancy impulsively turned. "How can you be so, so. . ." She couldn't go on. All her training disappeared and left a small girl, grieving for her lost sister.

"I thank God for every day of Timmy's life," came the surprising answer. "For five wonderful years I had a son who brought joy and gladness. His memory still does." A diamond drop slipped down one cheek and a gentle smile showed the strength God had supplied. "Nurse Nancy, as soon as I feel ready I'm going to apply for a child to adopt. Or if I can't get one, I'll do foster parenting."

Nancy started to speak then bit her tongue.

"Perhaps you wonder how I can think of it so soon. Actually, it's for Timmy. He would never want me to be lonely." She took in a long, quivering breath before adding, "Another child will never take my son's place but God has put many rooms in our hearts. I need to ready one for the child who needs me—the boy or girl God knows I need, as well."

Nancy left the house uplifted, knowing she would return again and again to the woman made strong through Christ Jesus.

"If his mother can react like that, why are you, a nurse, allowing the loss to tear you down?" she demanded of her mirrored image that night. The woman staring back at her had no answers, and the dark eyes hid secrets too painful to resurrect.

In late May, Damon did something about Nancy's problem. He waited for her at the end of her shift, casually mentioned various patients and their progress, complimented her on her continuing excellent work, and abruptly said, "There's a new Greek restaurant not far from here that has terrific food, even better than in the staff dining room. Would you like to try it?"

It caught her off balance. She rallied enough to nod, while her heartbeat quickened.

"Tonight?"

Goodness, but he didn't waste any time. "Why, yes. Give me an hour to change." She smiled at him.

"I'll do better than that. Let's make it seven so I can get to my apartment and check my answering service." A frown creased his forehead. "You know, of course, our date is subject to interruption; it goes with the job."

The corners of her lovely mouth tilted up and her laughter sounded like a chime of silver bells. "I do." It sounded too close to a wedding vow to leave her unmoved, especially when his dark gaze rested appreciatively on her.

"Pagers and answering machines are part of my life, too," she added.

"My boss leaves messages on the machine unless an emergency comes up, then he uses the pager," Damon told her. He grinned and added irrelevantly, "If you have a yellow dress, would you wear it, please? It makes you look like sunlight in a forest." He turned sharply on his heels and strode away.

Of all things! Nancy thought. *Dr. Damon Barton noticing colors and spouting poetic phrases!* Nancy stifled a giggle, feeling like a teenager and chastising herself for her unruly emotions. Yet in spite of laying out first a coral dress, then a white one, she met her date gowned in soft yellow that turned her skin to gleaming bronze and made her hair and eyes look even darker.

Damon merely said, "Thank you; you're lovely," but the look in his eyes betrayed much more than Nancy dared to interpret.

Two hours later, she sat back, replete and contented. Her escort's open admiration, the perfectly cooked meal, and quiet background music provided an atmosphere of total relaxation.

"Now we can talk," Damon announced after paying the bill and tipping a hovering waiter, who murmured thanks and whisked away dishes and crumbs.

"Isn't that what we have been doing?" Nancy laughed. "I thought we'd settled problems of world, state, and nation." She traced the shining pattern in the damask cloth with a slim forefinger, wishing the evening could go on and on.

"I'm glad to discover we share so many similar views," Damon told her. The timbre of his voice sent excitement skittering through her veins. "Added to our love for children and God, we really have a lot in common, don't we?"

She murmured assent, again feeling fluttery as a young girl on her first real date. Something stirred within her that had lain dormant for a long time, a feeling of being feminine, protected, cherished. The thought sent her lashes down to screen the expression she knew must be in her eyes. All the respect she had felt for the dedicated doctor mingled with wistful hope. *God, if someday I can marry a man as fine as Damon, I will find the security snatched away in my childhood.* The idea brought warmth to her smooth cheeks, and she scoffed at a grown woman pinning nebulous hopes on a casual first date.

If only she could get to know him better. To discover and alleviate the pain that often rested in his eyes when he wasn't laughing. The desire to give as well as receive help from this man leaped within her. Again, she scorned the idea. How could she give aid to another until she herself first became whole? "Physician, heal yourself,"* Jesus had said.

In a sudden about-face, Nancy took a giant stride toward freedom. Tomorrow she would begin the steps toward finding a qualified, Christian counselor. The decision brought a sense of incredible relief. She knew it showed in the snap of her voice, the quickened pace of

*Luke 4:23

her repartee.

At her door, Dr. Barton made no effort to detain her but clasped her hands in his, pressed them and said, "Next time will it be Chinese, Mexican, soul food, a thick steak, or. . .?"

"Any or all of the above," she told him airily. Yet after he'd left and she'd stepped inside her rose-and-white haven, she compared the shining-eyed vision in yellow with the sad-looking woman who too often had observed her from the mirror—and rejoiced.

It took a long time for Nancy to fall asleep. Her dates, rare from choice rather than lack of opportunity, seldom made more than a pleasant impression. Damon Barton's magnetic personality, slight tinge of mystery, and genuine concern had left their mark.

She also considered how to best find just the right counselor. Should she ask Damon? *No*. Her dark head moved on her pillow. She'd rather not tell him at this time. Nancy discarded several plans and finally decided to go straight to the hospital director, bypassing Dr. Paul, Jonica, and her other friends.

Glad that she had time off the next day, at last she slept, only to enter the nightmare world of her childhood. Leila, arms outstretched, crying for her year-older sister. Flames, dancing on the wall of the modest home Nancy, her mother, and sister occupied. Shouting. Curses. Prayers. A collage of terror. A blanket of gray smoke; streams of shining water. Then, a pit of blackness so deep the writhing woman felt she would smother.

Nancy awakened drenched with perspiration and stumbled to the shower. For a long time she stood under its cleansing stream, feeling horror sluice from her body and down the drain in a swirling motion. "God, I'm going to need all Your help," she whispered. Dried and clad in a fresh gown, she turned from her messy bed in distaste, snatched sheets and a blanket from her closet and parked on the comfortable living room sofa, as she had done countless times before. The next thing she knew, sunlight outside her window and the morning songs of a hundred birds bent on praising God awakened her.

An hour later she faced her director friend. "I've come to realize I need professional counseling to resolve a lot of things hanging over from childhood," she stated bluntly. "Who is the best and most Christian psychiatrist you know?"

"Nancy, I admire your courage in facing whatever dragons from the past are gnawing at you," he told her. "I think that perhaps you need a counselor more than a regular psychiatrist." He paused and his keen eyes surveyed her. "Do you have a male or female preference?"

She started to shake her head no, then reconsidered. Would another woman be better able to relate to her needs? "Perhaps a woman," she said.

He picked up the phone, dialed a number, and spoke into the receiver. "Helen, I have a special young woman here who needs exactly what you have to offer. Can you see her today?"

Nancy sat erect. *So soon?* She had resigned herself

to waiting weeks for an appointment.

"An hour from now? Good. Her name is Nancy Galbraith; she's one of our top nurses and her Pediatrics patients adore her. So does the rest of the hospital staff." He smiled at her. "Thanks. I owe you one." He cradled the phone. "You're set. And Nancy. . . ." Compassion filled his face. "Don't be afraid to tell Helen anything and everything. She's a deep well into which you can safely drop your confidences. She's also had a rather difficult time, although you'd never know it by her attitude toward life." The director scribbled on a piece of paper. "Here's her address. The door will be unlocked when you get there. Just walk in. Oh, her name is Helen Markel."

"Dr. Markel?"

A curious look crept into his eyes. "No, just Helen." He laughed at her obvious confusion. "You'll understand when you meet her."

Nancy wondered at his expression all the way to what she found was a private residence about a half-hour's drive from Shepherd of Love. The ranch-style home hugged the ground, surrounded by blooming impatiens in every color imaginable. A few choice roses nodded a welcome and a soft breeze fluttered birch leaves and played tag among a grove of evergreen trees. Surprise followed surprise. Nancy's automatic ring of the doorbell brought an instant, "Come in, Nancy" in a clear voice that stilled some of the tumult in her breast. She pushed open the door and stepped into the simplest, coziest home she had ever seen. Off-white walls served as a backdrop for soft pastel upholstered furniture. A woman slowly stood, reached for a cane and even more slowly came toward Nancy, right hand extended. "I am so glad you've come."

The last shred of fear evaporated. Who could dread a medium height, slender woman whose clear gray eyes were enhanced by smile wrinkles, whose sunny brown hair held silver threads here and there? *About forty,* Nancy figured, *but doesn't look it, because of the smooth complexion models of twenty would covet.*

"I-I think God sent me here." Nancy took Helen Markel's slim, capable hand. She noticed how strong a grip the other woman had and felt callouses that betrayed who did all the yardwork that made her home a place of beauty.

"I think so, too, although He sometimes has a way of using others to accomplish His purposes." Helen motioned her patient, who felt more like a guest, to a chair. Only then did Nancy realize the extent of Helen's lameness.

"A bad accident, ten years ago," she explained. "And in some ways the best thing that ever happened to me."

Nancy leaned forward, intrigued by the startling statement. "Really? I'd like to hear if you. . ."

"For every trial, there is a testimony." Helen leaned her head back against the soft rose of her chair and smiled. That smile curled into Nancy's heart like a coiled, purring cat. "To put it briefly, I'd pretty much lived for myself. After the car crash, it took months to put me back together. Doctors said I'd never walk again. I promised God that if He permitted me to do so, I'd turn my steps toward Him in all things. You see the results." She gestured at the cane. "I went back to school, got my master's in counseling. Yet the One I know is our Master Counselor is behind anything I can do. Actually, what I am best at is listening."

The last shred of apprehension melted. Nancy looked deep into the older woman's eyes and started at the result. Soul meeting soul; suffering meeting suffering. Hope stirred folded wings into a flutter. If anyone could help dispel the past, it would be Helen Markel.

"I don't quite know where to begin," she twisted her fingers together and confessed.

"With a cup of tea and a cookie, perhaps? Or would you prefer coffee or juice?"

"Juice if you have it. I'm a pushover for any kind. May I get it?"

Helen settled deeper into her comfortable chair. "Of course. I'll have apple juice, there's some open in the refrigerator, and the cookies are in the jar. Cups and plates in the cupboard above the sink; spoons in the drawers below."

Nancy grinned to herself while preparing the snack. "I suspect this is her way of making me relaxed and at home," she said, half under her breath. "Good psychology."

By the time they had finished the cold juice and Nancy

refused her fourth oatmeal-raisin cookie, the two women had become friends. Yet Helen permitted no serious talk until Nancy took the tray back to the kitchen and in spite of her hostess' protest, washed and put away the few dishes.

"All right, Nancy," she said when they were again seated across from one another. "Tell me about you. What's the earliest memory you have?"

Her visitor-patient thought for a moment. "The way my mother looked when Daddy left. Sad, yet with something in her eyes I couldn't understand—then. In later years, I identified the look as relief. I suppose it came with knowing that at least the terrible arguments went with him."

Helen's silent sympathy bolstered her courage.

"I must have been about four. My sister Leila was three." Her voice caught but she determinedly went on. "Mama must have gotten approved for low-income housing because a little later, the three of us moved into a house. I remember how excited I felt to have a real home and not just an apartment. We didn't have a lot, but Mama always told us we must thank God and help the 'poor' people—those in the development who had less than we did." A bright drop sparkled on her lashes.

"She made things fun. Although Mama worked hard, we still walked in parks and put crumbs out for the birds. We played with other children but Leila and I loved just being with Mama more than anything else." She paused, lost in memories. The off-white room faded from consciousness. Again she was four, then five, happy in her innocence with her little sister depending on her until the night her world ended. . . . .

"Nancy. Leila. Wake up!" A strong hand rudely shook her.

"Mama?" Nancy rubbed her eyes. "I can't see you." She took in a deep breath. "Why is it so hard to breathe?" She coughed and her eyes smarted. "Mama, why—?"

"Run outside, Nancy. Now!" Her mother snatched her from the bed she and Leila shared. "Don't stop for anything, no matter what happens. Get outside, you hear me?"

"Yes, Mama." Trained to instant obedience, she never questioned. Twisting herself free from Mama's quick hug, Nancy obeyed. Instinct stopped her in the doorway and she turned to look back. Her mother had scooped Leila from the huddle against the far side of the bed where she always curled into a ball.

Nancy screamed. Fire leaped between them, a wall of flame so hot the child shrank back. "Mama, where are you?" she wailed.

"Run, Nancy!" The hoarse command rang in the five-year-old's ears, along with Leila's frightened cries. In the heartbeat before Nancy fled, the curtain of flames lifted just enough for a final glimpse of her mother's agonized face, Leila's outstretched arms. Then with a demonic shriek, the fire roared hotter and higher. Nancy stumbled backwards.

"Run, darling. Mama loves you!" The beloved voice

echoed in her ears. She turned, tried to escape the pursuing heat. Something heavy struck her and she fell, screaming from the searing fever that spread across her shoulders and back.

A loud shout, strong arms, a voice saying, "It's all right, child; we'll get you out."

Nancy knew she was being carried but she struggled in the unfamiliar arms, regardless of her pain. "Mama. Leila. Please, get them!"

"More inside," the man who held her bellowed. He ran from the house, laid her on the ground, and started back to the house.

"God, help us," someone sobbed. The next instant, Nancy's dimming senses saw the home she loved collapse like a cardboard model beneath a powerful hand. Crashing, roaring, the inferno drove back those who sought to come close.

Nancy struggled to a sitting position, in shock until some of her pain subsided. She stared at the end of what had been their home, her and Leila's bedroom. A dark figure dashed across her field of vision.

For a single moment she saw his face, etched against the lurid light of flickering flames.

She never forgot. . . .

With a shudder, Nancy returned to the present and the quiet refuge of Helen Markel's peaceful home.

"My dear child, how you have suffered!"

The speaker seemed far away and Nancy bent her head down to let blood rush in and drive away her feeling of faintness. "I've never told anyone all of the story since I grew up," she said when she could speak. "The authorities tried to trace Daddy and failed. Fortunately, a kind neighbor took me in and kept me after I got out of the hospital until Child Placement found a foster home." A shadow swept over her heart. "The first of several, actually. The families were all kind but busy with their own children. As soon as I turned eighteen I was on my own. Good grades brought financial help. I took my nurses' training and at last came to Shepherd of Love, the first real home I'd known since the fire."

"You still carry scars."

"Yes. Plastic surgery took care of most of the physical scars."

"But not the inner ones." Helen leaned forward, bridged the space between the chairs and took Nancy's hands in her strong ones. The distraught nurse felt strength flow into her body. It gave her the courage to continue.

"The nightmare didn't end with our home lying there, rubble and a pile of ashes. The fire had been set, either deliberately or accidentally. The dark figure I saw against the flames turned out to be a teenage boy who lived not far from the development." Her hands tightened on Helen's, seeking consolation. "I never knew his name, just that after they released me from the hospital, a big man in a plain suit brought a lot of pictures. The boy had been in trouble before. They showed me photograph after photograph and every time I picked out the one I'd seen. . ." Her voice broke and she took a deep breath. "I think they put him in a home for juvenile offenders."

"You have never gone back to find out?"

Nancy slowly shook her dark head. "I couldn't bear to have a name with a face. It took everything in me just to go on living."

Helen's eyes brimmed, their clear gray softened with a fog of mist. "You became a Pediatrics nurse because of Leila?"

She nodded, too tired to speak.

"Perhaps it is the best thing you could have done. On the other hand, each time you lose a patient, it's like losing your little sister all over again."

Nancy felt the blood drain from her face. "How do you know?"

"My dear, you are flesh and blood, not a saint," Helen told her. "Right now you are feeling torn, aren't you? You want to go on saving life but wonder if it's worth the pain."

"You are a very wise woman," Nancy whispered. She freed her hands and fumbled for a tissue in her purse.

"Wisdom comes from God," Helen reminded.

"What shall I do? I really feel that God wants me to work with children, yet I don't know if I can continue."

four

Nancy restlessly stood and paced to the open window. The blooming flowers and their subtle perfume that drifted in cooled her hot cheeks. "What shall I do?" she asked.

"No one can tell you what to do but God. You must listen to your heart." Helen hesitated. "Nancy, have you forgiven the boy who set the fire?"

She turned, stared; red haze clogged her throat. "Forgiven?" She clenched her hands into fists; her nails bit into her palms. "He killed my mother and sister!" *How could this woman with the understanding eyes ask such a question?*

"Yet you are a Christian."

"I'm also human," Nancy flashed back. "Do you know what it's like, the nightmares, the—"

"I do." A world of sadness rested in the words.

"Forgive me, I'd forgotten." Nancy remorsefully crossed to Helen's chair and dropped to her knees beside it. "Helen, how could you forgive the driver who struck you?"

"By the grace of God."

Nancy flinched. She hadn't expected the direct answer. "I've tried to forget it," she whispered, "but I can't say I've forgiven."

"Perhaps you should." Helen flicked a tear off the kneeling woman's cheek. "Now, this is more than enough for today. Tell me, do you have lunch plans or can you stay with me?"

A little dazed by the abrupt change of subject, Nancy murmured, "Why, I can stay, if it's not an imposition." Helen patted her shoulder as if Nancy were still five. "I'll let you do the work."

A half hour later they sat down to a charming table sheltered from the bright sun by a large beach umbrella. A quickly mixed chicken salad, French bread buttered and warmed, a plate of richly red sliced tomatoes, and tall glasses of lemonade comprised their delicious meal. "I usually eat lunch out here and sometimes dinner," Helen said.

Nancy couldn't believe how hungry she felt. Or how empty of anything except this world within the world, so different from her daily routine. "I think heaven must be something like this." She breathed in the fragrance of roses and fought down the insane urge to put her head in Helen's lap and cry when the older woman bowed and asked God's blessing on the food, thanking Him for "the new friend He had sent." The feeling persisted and at first she found it difficult to swallow but Helen's quiet manner, the way she pointed out birds and butterflies did what nothing else could and her guest settled down and enjoyed the meal.

"When shall I come again?" she asked when she had no further excuse to linger. Again she had washed and dried the dishes and put them away.

"You may come any time of the day or night that you need me." Helen's keen eyes held compassion and sincerity. "Nancy, also know you will be in my prayers. Continuously. Give me your schedule for the next few days and every morning when you arrive for duty, remember that at that exact moment I'll be upholding you before the throne of God."

"I can never thank you, or Him, enough." She clasped Helen's hands in parting.

"I think you can, when you're ready."

Nancy pondered the strange remark all the way back to the staff residence. She took a long walk that brought her home in the midst of a glorious sunset fading to dusk. Just before she fell asleep later, the conversation that played through her mind reduced itself to a few words. Her own voice, saying: *I've tried to forget. . . I can't say I've forgiven.*

Helen, loving, gentle. *Perhaps you should.*

No flames tonight. No smoke. No crying child's voice. No nightmares. Just a soft voice that in the dark night hours changed to a different tone, yet always with the same words: *Perhaps you should.*

Nancy had been given enough food for thought to need time to digest it before going to see Helen again. She didn't report the results of the meeting to the hospital director either and she suspected that Helen would say nothing. She marveled at the instant confidence the servant of God who had been tested and found acceptable inspired. Could she someday do the same? The desire to care for far more than the physical bodies of her patients increased a hundredfold. She had always considered her duty to include caring for her patients' mental, emotional, and spiritual well-being as well as their physical. Now she saw clearly how crippled she still was by the past. Her soul cried out for freedom and always those significant three words *perhaps you should* lay just below the surface of her mind, ready to spring up in quiet moments.

Nancy rejoiced that she had Sunday off. She loved attending church. Shepherd of Love held several Sunday services and arranged schedules so the staff could attend one of them, but occasionally Nancy also liked going to a nearby church away from her work atmosphere. For this particular Sunday she prepared far more than usual. She reluctantly turned down a date with Dr. Barton and frankly told him she needed to do some soul-searching. She'd never forget the quick flare of happiness that lighted his black eyes and his, "I certainly understand."

She also fasted, starting with the Saturday evening meal and continuing her fast until after Sunday worship. "Lord," she prayed in the solitude of her room. "I feel I'm right on the verge of something wonderful and healing. I long to be whole. Please, open my heart and let Your Spirit take control."

Her heart thumped inside her chest when she took a seat in an obscure corner of the church the next morning. She saw groups from the hospital but preferred not to join them. All through the first hymn, she let her voice blend with the others in a song of praise. The invocation followed and then came a call to worship. Disappointment filled her. She had hoped that in some miraculous way the text for the morning would be aimed directly at her. The next moment she mentally chastised herself. Others here probably needed direction even more than she. Yet she sighed and opened her hymnal to the next song. The title leaped out at her. *FORGIVE OUR SINS AS WE FORGIVE. God, is this my answer?* Nancy couldn't get one word out as verse succeeded verse. What had the author, Rosamond E. Herklots, experienced to pen such powerful, applicable words that hurled themselves at Nancy like battering rams, asking how God's pardon can reach a heart that refuses to forgive; a soul that broods on wrongs and clings to bitterness.*

Shaken to the very core of her being, Nancy stared at the rapidly blurring page. She heard little of the sermon, although she sensed the rapt attention of those around her. Not until the congregation stood and repeated the Lord's Prayer together did she regain control. Yet when they came to the phrase, "forgive our trespasses as we forgive those who trespass against us," she broke. A terrible tumult left her nauseated, but through it her mute lips cried to her Heavenly Father for help. Memory of the peace in Helen's face when Nancy had demanded how she could forgive crept into the nurse's soul and the quiet reply, *by the grace of God.*

"I'll try, Lord," she brokenly whispered under cover of the closing hymn. She slipped out a side door, thankful for being able to escape unobserved. Bright sunlight

*paraphrased

greeted her among blue skies and a view of the Sound with its small, white-capped waves. Perhaps later in the day she would go to Helen Markel's and tell her of the seeds of peace she felt had been planted in her heart. For now, all she longed to do was find a spot where she could overlook the Sound in all its beauty and thank God.

Nancy hadn't escaped detection, as she thought. A few pews back and to one side of her, Dr. Damon Barton had surreptitiously watched her from the time she entered the sanctuary until the moment she left, every line of her body showing her wish to be alone. He could not intrude at such a time. He automatically smiled and greeted those about him, even while silently thanking God for the way he'd seen tension drain from Nancy's body during the service. Her frank explanation of turning down a date the evening before had shown she'd begun to come to terms with the things that loomed large and fearsome in her life.

If only he could share with her how Jesus longed to slay monsters, real and imaginary! Yet how many years had it taken for him to accept the fact and put the past where it belonged.

Damon wondered at how quickly the threads of respect and admiration he'd felt for Nancy Galbraith, R.N., had woven themselves into a web of attraction and something deeper. He cared far too much for her and had since the evening they'd shared at the Greek restaurant. A dozen times he had told himself, "Break it off while you can, Barton. You know there's no place for love in your life. You have vows to keep. Besides, what can you offer a woman like her?"

God, must this sense of unworthiness persist for the rest of Curtis' time on earth? Why should it be so hard for him to forgive himself when he knew beyond a shadow of a doubt that You forgave him long before he existed?

Damon shook his head to clear the cobwebs from his brain yet his heart plunged, thinking of the humiliation and invisible chains that still bound him. He tried to analyze them, to let go so God could finish His plan without interference from old hangups. He thought of the words of the song when he had observed Nancy's rigid stance. They applied to him, as well.

"'Old bitterness,' what an apt phrase," he muttered. Well, most of the bitterness had drained out of him. Yet the scar tissue sometimes grew tender from memories.

Fortunately for his peace of mind, when he reached his apartment, his answering machine held a message that drove speculation away.

"Damon, sorry to cut into your Sunday, but we have an emergency," Dr. Cranston's voice informed him. Incredibly, his voice shook, something Damon had never heard in the years they'd worked together. "My granddaughter Amy has had some kind of seizure. She's in Virginia Mason Hospital. Come as soon as you can."

Damon shot a prayer skyward. Four-year-old Amy, petite and charming, Dr. Cranston's only granddaughter, and the darling of his heart. What could have brought on a seizure? Damon's boss never tired of boasting how healthy Amy was. All the way to Virginia Mason, Damon continued to pray, as he did for each child he encountered. He also petitioned heaven for the right words to say. His heart fell. The Cranstons were morally upright people and attended church, yet in his association with them, Damon had seen no evidence of the abiding faith and trust in Jesus Christ that offered solace in troubled times.

An ashen-faced family met him. Their eyes silently pleaded for help. "You're to go right on in," Amy's mother said.

"I will do everything in my power to help," he promised. "In the meantime, you can help, as well. Ask God to give all who work with Amy His wisdom in discovering what's causing the problem." He left them staring after him but his heart felt light. He had said what he felt needed saying. Now they must choose.

Hours later he told a haggard Dr. Cranston the same thing. "Bob, we have to wait for the test results but you already know what I suspect."

"Brain tumor, possibly malignant," came through white lips. "I just don't see why it suddenly showed up. Amy's never showed symptoms before."

"It happens that way sometimes." Damon squared his shoulders. "There's a rush on the lab work so it won't be long."

"Every minute's an eternity." Robert Cranston shook his head. "From now on I'm going to have even more compassion on those who wait. I never knew it could be so hard."

"That's because we're in the middle of things, doing our job," Damon soberly told him. He gripped Cranston's arm. "I'm praying for Amy and for all of you." Shackles of reticence dropped off in the face of impending tragedy.

"Do you think if I promise God I'll try to be a better person that He will spare her?"

The eternal question, always with the same answer. "Bob, we can't bargain with God. We simply have to trust Him and allow His Spirit to guide us into what He wants from us."

Some of the hope in Cranston's face dimmed but he lifted his chin and in the remaining time before the X-rays came back, he comforted his family in a way Damon found beautiful.

"Just as we suspected. There's a small dark mass." Damon pointed to the film. "That's the culprit," he told the family who had gathered close to the lighted panel that held the X-rays.

"Take it out." Amy's mother never faltered.

"Right." Her father put an arm around his wife's shoulder. "Dad, do we need a specialist? I know you can't do it."

"Damon's as good as any in Seattle." The older doctor turned to his associate. "I'd rather trust Amy to him, and to his God, than anyone I know."

Dr. Barton blinked hard. Never in all his career had he felt more humble. "I'll be proud to operate as soon as we can arrange things," he told them. "Bob, you'll want to be there?"

"Yes, but I'd rather not assist. I'll just watch."

Damon thought he caught a faint, "and pray" but couldn't be sure. His heart leaped at the thought and even while he discussed details, made arrangements, and scrubbed for surgery, a constant prayer rose up that out of all this fear good things would come.

Amy looked small and defenseless when they wheeled her in. Her naked, shaved head lay still, her eyes closed. Dr. Cranston stepped close. "Amy, dear, Dr. Barton is going to take care of you. You're going to go to sleep and when you wake up, everything will be fine."

Her eyelids fluttered but she didn't rouse.

"She is, you know, no matter what happens," Damon said.

"I know. 'Of such is the kingdom of heaven'"* A white line formed around Cranston's mouth. "I just pray she'll pull through and stay with us." He strode away and when he returned, gowned and masked, all trace of personal involvement had disappeared.

From the time Damon lifted the scalpel and made his first incision, his Gibraltar-steady hand never wavered. He also had the assurance that so often came when he literally held life and death in his hand that One far stronger than He stood beside him, guiding, inspiring, healing. Yet the tumor lay in a tricky area. One slip meant disaster. Sweat beaded Damon's forehead above his mask and a nurse wiped it away time after time be-

*Matthew 19:14

fore the skilled surgeon carefully lifted the walnut-sized
tumor out and dropped it into the waiting receptacle.

"No sign of spreading," he rejoiced, voice steadier than
his heartbeat. "I believe it's benign." He began to close.

A barely discernible "Thank God" came from beneath
Dr. Cranston's mask, and the lightning glance of the doctors above the body of the child reflected joy and wonder.

With the resilience of the young, Amy Cranston healed
rapidly and Damon knew that in a few weeks she'd be
back playing and bringing even greater joy to her family
than ever before. He also noticed how his boss scrupu-
lously gave credit where due, frankly telling colleagues
and family he thanked God as well as Dr. Barton for
Amy's life.

One summer evening when Damon and Nancy had
gone for a drive after a quiet dinner, he parked in a spot
close to the edge of a hill that offered a view of a straw-
berry-ice-cream Mount Rainier on one side, the restless
Sound on the other.

"I believe the Holy Spirit is working in Bob's life as
never before," he exulted. In his excitement he captured
Nancy's hands and held them in both of his own. "So
often people turn to Him when tragedy strikes."

"Sometimes they turn away from Him," she reminded,
her face aglow with the setting sun's rays.

"Yes. Churches lose hundreds of members after shat-
tering experiences. Sometimes people don't know how
to meet hurting persons' needs, no matter how well-

intentioned they may be." He suddenly burst out in a
very un-Dr. Barton-like manner, "Don't you sometimes
long for a time when all the pain and hurt and sadness
are done away with forever?"

"Oh, yes." Her sensitive mouth quivered.

"Forgive me, Nancy. I don't mean to pry, but I've
been so engrossed with the Cranstons I haven't been able
to keep track of you." He searched her face for signs of
change. "You seem happier, more at ease, especially on
the wards."

"I am, Damon." A little breeze snatched at a dark
curl and worried it onto her cheek.

"I'm glad," he fervently told her.

"I didn't realize how much difference there was until
some of the children commented," she confessed.
"They've always been precious but yesterday a chubby
tot said, 'Nurth Nanthy, thankth for bein' tho thweet.'"

It took Damon a moment to translate her exact imita-
tion of the lisper's remark. When he did, he threw back
his head and laughed. "Well, Nurse Nancy, I'd also like
to thank you." His laughter died and he drew her closer.
Hands still clasped between them, he leaned forward
and kissed her full on the mouth. The second his lips
touched hers, Damon knew. Nancy Galbraith was the
woman he'd always looked for, never been sure would
come. More shaken at the revelation than he cared to
consider, he drew back and made a pretense of looking
at his watch. "We'd better go. It's getting late."

"Yes." Her monosyllable told him nothing. He longed

to pull her into his arms and let her spill every trial on his broad shoulders but he resisted. He might know exactly what he wanted but she couldn't, yet. He saw a look of hesitation in her eyes, a slight tremble of her lips. Rushing Nancy was the worst thing he could do. He steeled himself against her charm and when he walked her to her door, he forced himself to merely brush her cheek with his lips. "Dinner soon?"

"Soon." The door opened. She stepped inside and closed it. For some obscure reason, Damon felt like a foundling left on the steps of an orphanage, alone and lonely.

Whistling to rid himself of the idea, he slowly drove to his apartment. He scanned it with new awareness. If he married, someday, he didn't want an apartment, even this one. He wanted a house, a real home. It didn't have to be huge or ornate, although now that he'd finished paying off medical school debts money had ceased to be a real concern. He wanted a kitchen big enough for a rocking chair, the way he remembered from his own childhood. All the time-saving appliances he could buy. Whoever he married would in all probability be a nurse or doctor. She'd want to keep on with her career, at least until they had children.

Damon found himself resenting the word "whoever." Unless his affections changed with the instability of a weathervane, only Nancy Galbraith could sit across the table he imagined in their dining room, look up at him from a deep chair by a living room fireplace, laugh until the sound of her voice gladdened both home and hearth.

"Have you so soon forgotten all your intentions never to marry?" the ticking clock clacked.

Damon proudly raised his head. "I have not forgotten. I will still keep my vows and she will help me. God, I know You don't want me to do penance forever."

Yet some of his joy faded. Long before she ever could become Mrs. Dr. Barton, Nancy must learn things Damon had thought were buried forever. Anything else would be unthinkable.

"All these years. She'll understand. She's suffered, too." He threw himself down on a couch, stretched and yawned, but felt too keyed up to stay there. It hardly seemed possible happiness lay waiting around a turn or two in the rocky road life had been for him. Damon restlessly walked to the window. Far across the Sound, a thick fog had gathered. Its purple weight spread, lightened to gray where streetlights shone, remained black in the shadows. For some reason it depressed him. Perhaps because the evening had been so bright and beautiful and filled with promise.

Never one to allow weather to dominate his mood, he pulled the drapes and shut out the encroaching fog. An hour with a long-neglected medical journal, a chapter in his Bible, and his nightly talk with God left him more like himself. Still, just before falling asleep, Damon roused enough to wonder what the next day might bring.

five

After a satisfying, busy day, Damon unlocked his apartment door, feeling on top of his own little world. Love for Nancy Galbraith, a career of helping others, and knowledge he was making a difference in the world combined into contentment.

"'God's in His heaven, all's right with the world!'" he quoted from *Pippa Passes*. "Robert Browning, I salute you. It's summer, not spring, and evening rather than morning, but everything else,. . ."

He abruptly stopped, raised his head, and sniffed. *Smoke!* Dropping the medical bag he always carried to the entryway hall, he dashed into the living area. A premonition of disaster caught at his throat and was replaced with a familiar sickness he had prayed never to feel again.

"Hello, Damon."

Dr. Barton's peace shattered, the same way fragile Christmas tree ornaments break into a hundred, irretrievable pieces when dropped.

The man lolling on the couch, cigarette in one hand, raised an eyebrow, twin to Damon's. His face, also like that of the slowly icing statue in front of him, contorted into a malicious smile. "Some welcome for your long-lost older brother." He took a final puff on his cigarette, stubbed it out in a cup evidently purloined from the kitchen and sprang to his feet in a fluid motion.

"Better than you deserve." Dr. Barton stood absolutely still. "What are you doing here, Curtis?" Body rigid, he surveyed his brother. Twenty years hadn't changed him much, except the boy he had been now stood before him as a man, enough like Damon's mirror image to be a twin. Closer examination denied the likeness. Harsh lines, faint signs of dissipation marred what could have been an open, likable countenance. Curtis Barton looked years older than his brother, although barely twelve months separated them in age.

"Well?" Damon demanded.

"Things got hot in L.A." Curtis lifted his shoulders in a careless shrug. "I decided to, shall we say, move my scene of operations to Seattle." A mocking gleam lit the midnight-black eyes. "Figured I could bunk in with you until I see where the action is."

Anger Damon thought he had conquered when he'd turned his life over to God swept through him. "Get out."

"You don't mean that!" Shock erased the sardonic, taunting expression. Something flickered in Curtis' eyes.

"I never meant anything more in my life. Get out."

Curtis turned curiously pale beneath his dark skin. A curse ripped the tension between them. "You can't just throw me out." Another curse. "You're my brother."

Damon laughed in his face, a laugh so unlike his usual self even Curtis took a step backwards. "Watch me. I've spent most of my life feeling ashamed and guilty because of you. Don't think you can come waltzing in here and lay a guilt trip on me because you're in trouble. You are, aren't you?"

A look akin to fear came into the older man's face. "Big trouble."

"What did you do, rat on someone?"

Curtis licked his lips. He furtively glanced at the door. "Keep your voice down, will you? Yeah, I turned state's evidence in a murder trial and the gang's out to get me." Stark terror showed in the way his hands shook. "I knew everything was going down and saved my skin. Anything wrong with that?" Some of his defiance returned. "Would you rather have me be a TV headline?"

Damon, who had looked on incredible suffering, felt sick. It was the same way he'd felt years before when a neighborhood bully hit him in the stomach. All the anguish he had fought so long to overcome stood embodied in his brother. "How did you get in?" he hoarsely asked. "First, how'd you find me?"

"I can still read the phone directory." An unpleasant smile curved Curtis' lips upwards. "Have to admit, I didn't expect to find you a doctor. 'You've come a long way, baby,' as the ad says."

In that moment Damon thoroughly hated him. *God, why does this specter I buried and left behind rise from the past?*

"I remembered we used to pass for one another." Curtis laughed suggestively and Damon's hurting heart leaped. "Figured I'd trade on it. Came in, smiled at the manager, female, fortunately, and said for some reason I didn't have my key. She fell all over herself letting me in." He rolled his eyes and simpered, "'Any time, Dr. Barton. We're all just so proud of the wonderful work you're doing. My friend works as a nurse and she says you're the best young children's specialist in Seattle.'" Curtis dropped his falsetto. "She also got off a lot of stuff about what a fine Christian example you are. I guess it doesn't stretch to your prodigal brother."

The sneer sent a wave of blood into Damon's face. "Give me one reason why it should."

Curtis dropped back to the couch and lit another cigarette.

"Put it out," Damon ordered. "I don't permit smoking in here. By anyone." For a moment he thought Curtis would argue and felt inward relief when he sullenly extinguished the burning cigarette, muttering a curse.

"That doesn't go here, either," Damon told him sharply. "This is my home and it's dedicated to God, the same way I am. Nothing is allowed here that will displease Him."

"Don't preach at me," Curtis flamed. "I got enough of that rot when I was a kid."

Damon relentlessly told him, "Just remember one thing. God is the head of this household. He isn't leaving. If you can't respect that, you are." He saw the flare of hope in his brother's eyes and quickly added, "I'm not saying you can stay here. Just that while you're here at all, you'll play by my rules."

"Tough talk for a Christian. I thought they were supposed to be meek and forgiving." Curtis never could resist the urge to heckle, to pin an opponent as mercilessly as a butterfly marked for mounting. He yawned and stretched. "What's in it for you, anyway? I get along fine without Sunday School stories and pious hymn-singing hypocrites."

"Oh? Then just why are you here?" Damon softly inquired. "If you're doing so great, why are you running scared and using me to hide behind?"

Curtis sat up straight. For a moment Damon thought he would leap off the couch and hit him. "Listen, punk, I don't hide behind anyone. All I need is a loan. Bread. Bucks. Don't tell me you haven't got them, a successful doc like you."

Damon shook his head, braced his feet, and prepared for battle. "Sorry, big brother. I told you five years ago when you called I'd never bail you out again. I meant it then. I still mean it. You got yourself in this mess; it's up to you to get out of it any way you can."

"You won't like the way I do it," Curtis threatened. His eyes turned to obsidian.

"So what's new? I haven't liked any of what little I knew about your life style in the last twenty years."

"Why, you. . ."

Damon saw the way Curtis bit back an obscenity and the effort it took. More than anything so far, it pointed up how desperate Curtis really was. He would never take anything off anyone. Again Damon felt sick. *How far did being a brother's keeper go?*

Did Curtis, with the same ability to catch his brother's wavelength he'd had since childhood, discern the thought? His lips curled, lips that could have been handsome if not twisted into cynicism most of the time. "The way I remember it, when the prodigal son came home, his father threw a party for him, killed the fatted calf, all that stuff."

Damon didn't give an inch. "The day you return to your Heavenly Father, He will rejoice and welcome you. I'm not God, just the brother who,. . ."

"Don't throw the past up to me. I won't have my little brother strutting around all holy and righteous before the poor, lost sinner!" He ground his teeth until it sounded loud in the quiet room. "Are you going to help me, or not?"

"As the old saying goes, 'there's good news and bad news.'"

Curtis looked wary.

"The bad news is, no loan. No bucks. No staying here with me."

For a single instant, Curtis looked like a pricked balloon. He recovered so quickly Damon couldn't be sure he had actually seen the look of despair and fear in his eyes. "And the good news?"

Years receded. A small Damon who adored his brother danced in Dr. Barton's mind. Love he had thought gone forever, even after forgiveness came, roughened his voice. "You have the right to know why I won't give you money or let you stay here." He took in a long breath, praying that somehow the Holy Spirit would penetrate the layers of murk that bound Curtis. "Five years ago I realized part of your problem was me."

"Wha-at. . . ." Curtis' mouth hung open.

Damon nodded. "A long time ago when I became a Christian and asked God to forgive me for the way I hated what you'd done to me, I also put you in His hands."

Curtis squirmed, started to speak.

"Wait! If you've never listened to anything before, you'll listen now." The words rang. Damon felt a surge of power and the desire to make Curtis understand he stood on the brink of destruction. "Even though I told God I would accept whatever He chose to allow in your life in order to bring you to Him, when you called pleading for help, I couldn't stand the thought of you in prison, or sick or in trouble. Maybe some of it was pride, or the way I felt dirty that my own brother had chosen to involve himself in unspeakable things. I never knew all of what you'd done. I didn't want to know. It hurt too much. I guess a spark of what Mother taught us about being a family still lived. Anyway, in spite of promising God to accept His will, I stepped in." Damon stared blindly at his nemesis, the figure he had loved, hated, idolized, and seen fall.

"So, I sent money, whatever I could. A couple of times it meant borrowing from the bank and doing without necessities."

Curtis sent a significant look around the tastefully

decorated apartment. "It sure looks like you're poverty-stricken," he sarcastically said.

Damon ignored him. "The bottom line is, I realized the last time I stepped in had to be just that: the last time. Otherwise, my rescuing you meant all God's allowing you to be in misery meant nothing. You'd simply go on believing no matter what happened, I'd be here to take care of it."

"So you'll let your own brother rot in jail or be killed." Disbelief erased every trace of swagger.

The hardest words Damon ever had to say fell slowly and quietly from pallid lips. "Curtis, I have no choice."

The man on the couch sagged. His lips pulled back like a beast at bay. "Tell this to that God of yours. Anyone, God or not, who turns brother against brother, is pretty rotten. When you get a call to come identify me in the morgue you can remember who put me there." He stood and lurched toward the door.

Damon longed to rush after him, to give in. What did a vow mean if, as Curtis said, his brother's life hung in the balance? Yet a little voice inside reminded, *if you give in now, then all the agony of leaving him in God's hands is for nothing. God, was any man ever so torn?* Damon found his voice just before his brother opened the door and vanished. "It isn't I who put you where you are. It's you."

The door slammed. Damon heard footsteps pound away then dwindle into nothingness, the way Curtis' life had dwindled into sin. Unashamed tears fell and the doctor, made strong to do what he believed God required dropped to his knees, pouring his heart out until a measure of uneasy peace returned, but without a trace of his earlier joy.

Time after time in the next few days Damon found himself mired in doubt. It took every ounce of strength he possessed to continue with his duties and wear an outward calm for the sake of his little patients. He avoided Nancy. A dozen times he reached for the phone to call then let his hand drop. How could he even consider involving her in his life when that life carried the albatross of a brother gone wrong? What if those who surely would trace Curtis discovered his brother? They would have no scruples in using any person even vaguely associated with their prey in order to get to him. For her sake, at least until, until what? In any event, he could not expose her to possible harm.

The strain took its inevitable toll. Damon dreaded coming home after work. Not that he expected Curtis to be there. Their final confrontation had killed that fear. A man as proud as his brother, once he saw the truth, would never beg. The answering machine became a foe. Damon nerved himself to play his daily messages, always with the words, *when you get a call to come identify me. . .* lurking in his brain. He had replayed the scene again and again, coming up with items he hadn't realized had registered at the time. Such as the lack of street language in Curtis' speech. Other than the taboo profanity and smothered obscenities, he had spoken as easily and well as Damon. It brought up questions. Surely Curtis couldn't have been all these years in the gang scene and not picked up the way they talked.

Determined to discover exactly what had driven him from L.A. to Seattle, Damon arranged with Dr. Cranston for a few days off. He flew directly to L.A. and went straight to police headquarters.

"I'd like to find out about a murder," he told the office who asked what he wanted.

"A murder? How about a dozen? A hundred?" The officer stared suspiciously at him. "Who are you, anyway?"

"Damon Barton, M.D., Seattle." Damon handed over a business card and received a noncommittal grunt in return. "A man I know, also named Barton, recently turned state's evidence in a murder trial. I need to know what happened." He silently prayed for God to open the way.

A half-hour later he left the station, heart in his shoes. In spite of the wealth of evidence against him, Damon had hoped Curtis exaggerated his latest crime. He hadn't. He'd saved his skin by fingering two men in a drive-by shooting, one he witnessed (according to him) from a storefront window. The killers insisted Barton had been with them but Curtis had miraculously slipped through the net and his police record contained small stuff only. The DA had willingly cut a deal, letting the little fish swim away while he went for the sharks and got a conviction plus a life sentence for the shooter and a prison term for the accomplice.

"Your friend," the officer raised a skeptical eyebrow, "was lucky. Tell him that from L.A.P.D. You might also tell him the two he informed on have friends. Lots of them."

"I will." Damon thanked the officer and headed outside. Even the L.A. smog smelled better than the atmosphere of sin and misery inside. He caught the earliest flight to Seattle he could book and considered all the way home how to warn Curtis, even though his brother was already fully aware of his perilous situation.

"Did you say something?" the flight attendant inquired.

Damon shook his head. He hadn't realized he'd quoted Romans 6:23 aloud. "*For the wages of sin is death. . .*" He mentally finished, "*but the gift of God is eternal life through Jesus Christ our Lord.*" Suddenly, he understood more fully how Jesus felt when He wept over Jerusalem. How could men, women, even children, rush heedlessly toward spiritual as well as physical death, laughing gaily and spurning the only One who offered hope? Many didn't have the excuse of not knowing. TV and billboards, churches with spires toward heaven that served to remind those who rushed past their open doors persons like Dr. and Mrs. Paul Hamilton and the others at the Shepherd of Love Sanctuary in the inner city; all offered a clear message of the way to salvation.

Damon bowed his head and prayed again that no matter what it took, God would one day bring Curtis to his knees and soften a heart that appeared to be made of lead, like the bullets in the little man's gun.

A sense of the need to find his brother and talk with him again sent Dr. Barton to the streets of Seattle. Without any idea of where Curtis might be, Damon walked aimlessly but with a knowledge God could help him find the one soul among thousands. His faith proved justified a week later. He came face-to-face with Curtis on Broadway.

"Hello, little brother."

"Hello." He scanned the other for signs of hunger, secretly wondering how he had managed to survive.

With uncanny insight, Curtis sneered. "I'm eating. Never fear. Doing just fine without help." He motioned significantly toward an obviously-new custom suit and expensive shoes.

"Where did you get them?" Damon felt stretched to the breaking point.

"I have ways." Curtis flicked ashes from his cigarette and walked toward a crouching black limo purring at the curb.

"Wait." Damon reached a long arm, caught his brother's shoulder and lowered his voice. "L.A.P.D. says to tell you,. . ."

"You fool!" Curtis' voice went low and deadly. "What do you know?"

"Everything. I went down and found out."

Curtis backed off, a flicker in his eyes Damon couldn't read. "Keep away from me. Get it?" He raised his voice in a stream of profanity that turned the air blue, wheeled, and was swallowed by the limo that glided away like a great jungle cat with its prey.

"Drugs," Dr. Barton whispered. "The only way he could wear that suit. Wonder who owns the limo?" He strained his eyes to catch a license number but the distance stopped him. Besides, what good would it do to know? He could do nothing to save Curtis without further endangering him. Caught in a web woven by Satan and inhabited by his followers, Curtis must choose to extricate himself or remain trapped forever.

Damon reached his apartment, ignored the blinking answering machine, and headed for his shower. Oh, to let the hot water pour over him and make him clean. He thought of the day he was baptized and of the moment he came out of the water. He had felt clean, then. As if every dark and ugly thing in life washed from body and soul had left him. Yet no one could live in today's world and be totally free of its smirch. Some tried. Not for him, the way of withdrawal. The same world that repelled him needed his skills and his witness.

He stayed in the shower for a long time before toweling himself and donning fresh clothing from the skin out. A rueful smile came to his lips when he dropped his dirty clothes in the hamper and hung his wet towel to dry. "Too bad we can't send out hearts and souls to the laundry when they get stained," he muttered.

Nothing on his answering machine required his immediate attention, so Damon settled down with his Bible. He'd found it the sure way to relieve tension and bring back hope. Yet now the scriptures blurred a little. The way he had chosen seemed hard and long. Was there really any danger to him or to Nancy, if he renewed their friendship? He knew from the quick way she glanced at him when he ran into her at Shepherd of Love she wondered why he had stopped calling. "God," he prayed. "I love her so much. You know I will never do anything that might hurt her. Guide and direct us both. In Jesus' name, amen."

Peace came slowly, on soft, kitten feet that tucked themselves into a sense of all-rightness. An hour later, Damon looked at the ticking clock. Only ten. He dialed, waited. When Nancy answered he said, "It's Damon. If you have tomorrow off, will you go to church with me?" He gripped the phone, tense as the first time he had called a teenage girl and asked for a date. She responded. He cradled the phone, and chided himself for the spurt of gladness that spread throughout his body at the thought of their worshipping together in the morning. "Go slowly," he warned himself. "Don't try to run before the Lord."

Yet the steady pound of his heart and the anticipation he felt were completely out of proportion to the fact Nancy had only agreed to a date for church.

six

When Damon kissed her for the first time, Nancy Galbraith longed to respond with her whole heart. She couldn't. Suppose it meant nothing more to him than a pleasant way to let her know he liked her? She shrank from the thought, especially when Dr. Barton huskily said, "We'd better go. It's getting late."

"Yes." Nancy said quietly beside him on the drive home, outwardly calm, inwardly quivering like an aspen leaf in the presence of her sweetheart, the wind. A great feeling of longing assailed her, the desire to be more to Damon than a good friend and someone to date. *God, is this of You?*

"Dinner soon?" he asked at the door, after brushing her cheek with his lips.

"Soon." She stepped inside, closed the door, and leaned against it. His sure footsteps faded and died but the sense of his compassion did not. Nancy flung herself on the bed, heedless of crushing her dress. She flipped on her back, clasped her hands behind her head, and stared at the ceiling. Surely she was old and mature enough to discern between friendship and growing attraction. She remembered the look in Damon's dark eyes and attempted to analyze it. *Admiration? Yes. Caring? Obviously.*

Love? She stopped short in her dissection. She must not read into the dedicated doctor's attentions more than existed.

"What do I really know about him?" she whispered. Her active brain presented the facts: is a noted physician and surgeon, loves children, appears to be a strong Christian.

Nancy's eye widened. Why would she qualify Damon's Christianity by saying "appears to be"? Did she doubt his sincerity? He had no reason to pretend, did he? Her heart shouted the affirmation of his integrity while her mind tried to remain objective.

"Stop playing psychiatrist and get ready for bed," she ordered herself. Yet far into the night she restlessly shifted between waking and sleeping, more troubled about Dr. Barton and her growing feelings for him than she wanted to admit.

She awakened to a new day filled with bright hope. Her mirrored image's eyes sparkled and she laughed out loud. "Can't wait to see him, can you? You're worse than a teenager." The chastisement resulted in her bypassing the yellow uniform in favor of a soft pink that made her look like a blooming Queen Elizabeth rose.

Her small patients' chorus, "Nurse Nancy, you're all pink!" gladdened her heart and when the time came for Dr. Barton to arrive, she took three deep breaths and anticipated the moment with both pleasure and a little fear.

"Nancy," a fellow nurse called to her. "Dr. Barton is

going to change his visitation hours due to some things that have come up. He will be in during the evening shift for a time."

Nancy's spirits hit the ground with a heavy thud. She could feel her face burn. Humiliated, she averted her gaze to hide her agitation. So she had been right. Damon evidently didn't want to see her. The kiss had meant nothing. A new thought pounded at the door of her heart and no barring could keep it out. Evidently he feared she might take his spontaneous affection to mean more than he intended. What if, with his trained understanding, he had seen how much it meant to her? She tensed, forced herself to relax. No one, and that meant Dr. Barton above all others, must see her distress. With a quickly whispered prayer for strength, she forced hands, feet, mind, and heart to go about her duties. Perhaps her inner turmoil and suffering gentled her voice and added even more skill than usual to her ministrations. In any event, the most fractious children settled at the sound of her instructions.

Each day brought more assurance that Damon regretted his attentions to her. Nancy's phone rang often, but never with the voice she longed to hear. The few times she saw Dr. Barton he acted brusque and wore an abstracted manner. Once Nancy thought she caught a look in his eyes she could only describe as pleading, but his continued avoidance of her and his cold demeanor when they met quickly erased that impression.

On the other hand, her friendship with Helen Markel

grew with every visit to the charming, flower-surrounded home. Nancy found herself dropping by at every opportunity. She and Helen sometimes just sat in the garden, quietly chatting or silently absorbing the peace. "You're one of the nicest gifts God has given me," she wistfully told her hostess.

A tinge of pleased pink touched the older woman's face and her clear gray eyes misted. "I've been thinking the same about you, my dear." The look that passed between them spoke volumes.

"You never push." Nancy watched a bee, tipsy from pollen, rise and fly in an uneven path to another flower. "You just allow me to share when I feel I can and otherwise remain still."

"One of my favorite scriptures is, 'Be still, and know that I am God,'" Helen softly quoted.

"Psalm 46:10. It's one of mine, too." Yet Nancy shifted restlessly in her chair. "It's hard to find time or a place to be still in today's chaotic world."

"One of the lessons I learned from the accident was that stillness can be internal and not depend on where we are." She suddenly laughed and Nancy's mouth involuntarily tipped up at the cheerful sound. A squawking blue jay perched on the edge of the birdbath, cocked his head to one side, cast a beady glance at the two humans who dared invade his kingdom, and scolded them roundly.

"Despite what Mr. Jay says, it's true," Helen insisted. "The reason I laughed is because even though I believe we carry much of our peace with us, I also made sure this garden would be here whenever I, or others, need it."

"It is a balm to the eyes and soul," Nancy confirmed. She drew in a fragrant breath of flower-scented air. "I leave here feeling I am a new woman." She paused and lowered her voice. "I-I haven't told you before, I wanted to make sure I could carry through, but the Sunday after I first came here, something happened." She sketched in her day of fasting, the way Helen's words about the need to forgive had haunted her. She brokenly repeated her prayer of petition to be whole. Awe in her voice and tears shining in her beautiful eyes, Nancy told how the words of a hymn had sunk deep in her soul with their cutting message of the need to forgive.

"I could only tell God I'd try to forgive the boy who set the fire," she whispered.

"And since then?" Loving concern robbed the question of impertinence.

"I have been more at peace, at least until. . ." She stopped. Not even to Helen could she confess her feelings for a doctor who daily made clear by his actions he had no interest in her.

If Helen caught an underlying message she gave no sign. "The most wonderful thing about forgiveness is what it does for the wronged person," she said. Her face shone with certainty. "I felt so chained until I could freely forgive."

"I've experienced some of that," Nancy admitted. Her

taut fingers, that had tightened on her chair arms during her recital, relaxed.

"If you will continue practicing what I believe is the healing art of forgiveness, you will discover freedom beyond verbal expression." The tranquility in Helen's face spread into Nancy's heart, the way spilled oil stretches into an ever-widening pool, coating whatever it touches.

"Nancy, when have you had a vacation?"

The abrupt change of subject startled her. "Why, I took a few days off last fall."

"I don't mean a few days. I mean a real vacation. One where you got away from your daily routine and did something completely different." Helen raised an eyebrow and waited.

"Never." She tried to smooth over the bald remark by explaining, "What with training and work and special cases needing me, there just hasn't been a good time."

"There never is, for those who are dedicated to what they do. Yet you cannot go on and on giving without time to be refilled. It's like draining a glass of lemonade and expecting to keep on pouring out when everything is gone. I suggest you think seriously about setting a specific time for vacation, two weeks at the minimum. Experts who study fatigue problems among workers say one of the greatest mistakes persons make is taking only one week vacation at a time. It takes two, perhaps three days to shove aside job-related stress and thoughts of what you left undone. Two to three days before you go back, your mind always fastens on getting back to work.

That doesn't leave enough time in between." Helen leaned forward with a no-nonsense-about-being-indispensable glint in her eyes. "This isn't a suggestion, Nancy. It's an order. I'm speaking as your professional counselor rather than as your friend and I'm telling you to get away."

"I don't know where to go or what to do." The spurt of excitement over just walking away from her problems died. How could she leave her biggest problem, herself?

Helen threw up her hands and grimaced. "You remind me of the classic story about a famous man, I don't remember who, but the tale goes he became exhausted from working. He told his wife he had to get away. Like you, he didn't know where to go or what to do."

Nancy listened to the story carefully. She had found that Helen followed Jesus' teaching pattern and used parables to make important points.

Helen went on. A twinkle rested in her eyes and a smile lurked at the corners of her mouth. "Being a wise woman, the wife gave a fine suggestion. She told her husband, 'I agree that you need time off. Now, you must think of the place you'd rather be than any other place in the world. You must decide what you love most in life and that's what you should do.'"

"And?" Nancy held her breath.

The corners of Helen's mouth went down. "The famous man went back to work!"

Nancy stared, then a chuckle burst from her throat and

changed to a full-scale laugh.

Helen kept a straight face although her eyes gave away her inner mirth. "I wouldn't want to say you resemble the man in the story. . . ." A quirked eyebrow and droll expression wordlessly completed her sentence. She rose, slowly walked to her guest, and patted her hand. "Think about it, Nancy. Being married to your work is good to a point but not when you become so involved, you have no other life."

The seed fell into fertile ground. A short time later, Nancy signed up for two weeks' vacation. The prompt way her request was granted made her wonder if Helen Markel had dropped a hint in the right place. She shrugged. It didn't matter. Now that she'd taken the first step, the idea of getting away for a time intrigued her. She considered and rejected the idea of asking Patty, Lindsey, or Shina to accompany her. Even their cheerful presence would remind her of Shepherd of Love and for two wonderful weeks she intended to shelve both hospital and her own problems, including the elusive Dr. Barton who continued to act distant and inattentive when they met by chance.

"If it weren't that you need to get clean away, I'd offer you my home for your vacation," Helen told her. "There's a special conference and I'm flying to California to attend. I'll also visit various friends." She drew her brows together. "Nancy, I've had a key made for you. There's no reason to wait for me to let you in even when I'm home." She smiled at the younger woman. "You're as dear as a daughter. If I weren't afraid you would lean too much on me and not become the person God wants you to be, I'd invite you to live with me."

Nancy blinked and swallowed hard. "Thanks, but you're right. I would rely too much on you when what I need to do is continue learning to rely on God." A vague idea flitted through her brain. "I plan to go to either the beach or the mountains, maybe both, for the first part of my vacation. If I get rested and want to come back before the two weeks are up, may I stay here?"

"Absolutely." Helen put on a ferocious scowl that didn't deceive Nancy. "No cheating, though. I don't want to come back and find out you've been here all the time, on call if the hospital thinks it needs you."

"I won't even give them your phone number," Nancy promised, then shivered, not knowing why. Nothing could be less threatening in the entire world than Helen Markel's quiet home and garden.

With each passing day, Nancy realized how wise her friend and mentor had been to insist that she take time off. Her heart bounced at the thought of long hours walking the beach. The crashing waves would surely drown out the cries of children who pleaded for her help. The clear, blue ocean and matching sky would offer a chance for her to regain perspective by their very timelessness. Sandpipers, plovers with their short, hard-tipped bills and more compact build, screeching gulls, scuttling crabs, and sand dollars; all fringe benefits to encourage beach tramps in fresh, salty air that promoted appetite and healthful sleep.

For several days she didn't see Dr. Barton. A real pang shot through her. What had happened to their growing friendship? She had felt it so real. He didn't appear at all on the Saturday that marked her final work day before vacation. She sighed and left the ward in a saddened mood. Fourteen days from now when she returned, hopefully rested and ready to take up her numerous and taxing duties, Pediatrics wouldn't be the same. Some of her patients would have been released; one or two taken home to their heavenly Father. The rush of feeling that rose inside her again confirmed her need to get away. A nurse who became too attached to her patients harmed rather than helped them, as well as herself. She slowly walked to her suite. Should she change her plans and start for the coast tonight? Although the snug cabin she had rented through a travel agency was reserved starting Monday, she could certainly find somewhere to stay.

She shook her head. Maybe not. With the continuing good weather, people flocked to the beaches. Before she decided exactly when to leave she'd learned from the travel agent how necessary it was to get firm reservations. "A lot of people end up sleeping in their cars or on the beach," he warned. Nancy had paid for the first week with the understanding that if she wished to stay longer, she'd let him know no later than Friday morning. He'd have no trouble getting someone else for the cabin, should she plan to leave on that Sunday.

Unwilling to cling to the hospital, she ordered in a

small pizza and large salad rather than going to the staff dining hall. She munched and watched a game show, in itself a rare occurrence, and ended up bathed and in bed by ten o'clock, propped up against her pillows and anticipating the joy of reading herself to sleep. No alarm to set tonight! She'd get up when she pleased, go to church, and let the rest of the day take care of itself.

The sharp ring of the bedside phone jangled into her plans. For a moment she felt tempted to just let it ring. Duty won over desire and she picked it up.

"Hello?"

"Nancy, it's Damon. If you have tomorrow off, will you go to church with me?"

A hundred thoughts milled in her mind, a hundred feelings in her heart. Just when she had begun to accept his disinterest, Dr. Barton crashed back into her life. Her lip curled. She should give him a flat no and get on with her vacation.

She couldn't do it. After a brief pause she heard her voice, controlled and even, agreeing to accompany him to church. A quick agreement on the time and a click ended the conversation. It did not end Nancy's dilemma. "Why did you say yes?" she demanded out loud. "Fine way to start getting away from everything." She thought of the way he sounded, not at all like the reserved Dr. Barton who had shied away from her in Pediatrics except when necessity demanded that they discuss patients' care. He had sounded more like the Damon who had showed his concern and genuine liking for her, the Damon she realized she had grown to love.

Seeing into her own heart also explained why she had felt so hurt when he rejected her. Or had he? Could there be another reason for his coldness?

"Well, God," she said. "There's no better place to get things straightened out than in church." Happiness curled into her heart like a sun-warmed blanket. She put aside her unread book, switched off her bedlight, and closed her eyes. To her surprise, when she opened them again, an errant ray of sunlight had sneaked in around the curtain, heralding a new and special Sunday.

Damon arrived promptly. Nancy saw the quick look he gave her and her heart fluttered. She hadn't dared wear yellow, but knew her white suit, scarlet shoes, and matching scarf became her.

"I'm glad you are free," he told her. His gaze said much more.

She bit her tongue to keep from affirming her own gladness and contented herself with a smile.

"Nancy, would you mind going to a different church this morning?" A kind of urgency laced his simple question.

"Not at all. What do you have in mind?"

"You know Dr. Paul Hamilton, Jonica, and Paul's father have recently completed a chapel at the Shepherd of Love Sanctuary downtown?"

"I hadn't heard." A little quiver ran through her. She hadn't yet gone down to the inner city to serve. Not until she fought and vanquished her own childhood dragons would she be able to work with those who were less fortunate.

"Paul's going to speak this morning and several of those the Clinic serves have promised to come." Damon's fine hands tightened on the steering wheel. "I thought it would be nice to give him some moral support."

"Why, yes. I haven't seen Jonica for a time, what with. . ."

A speeding car cut in front of them and sliced across Nancy's explanation about her upcoming vacation. She braced herself and noticed how capably her escort swung their vehicle out of harm's way. The near accident successfully drove all else from mind and Damon's quick, "Hope the Seattle Police get that menace off the streets," further sidetracked her.

After they had parked in a lot next to the newly-constructed chapel, Nancy said, "Maybe I'll be overdressed."

"You look fine to me," he assured her but she shook her head and resolutely untied the bright scarf, then reached into her carryall bag and pulled out a pair of plain white pumps with flat heels. "I'll wear these. I didn't know what plans you might have for this afternoon so I tucked them in." She slipped them on and smiled at him. "Not so dramatic as red."

"You're a very special and considerate woman, Nancy Galbraith." He got out, locked his door, and came around to open hers. "I'm proud to know you."

His words stayed with her while they entered the plain

building with its simple furnishings and white walls. The chapel's only claim to beauty lay in the richly-colored window in the east wall. Damon ushered Nancy into a pew on the west side and seated himself beside her. About twenty others sat scattered in the room, clean, but showing signs of poverty. Nancy felt then a sudden brightening and glanced at the window beyond Damon. Sunlight poured through, making a living mosaic of the colors.

She turned her gaze to Damon, and saw his face, outlined against the sun-glorified stained glass window.

She never forgot the moment. Her heartbeat slowed. She felt blood drain from her face and sat as it turned to stone. Twenty years receded and a long-remembered face etched against the light of flickering flames rose in her mind. A boy's face.

Nancy closed her eyes against the swell of pain, and reopened them to confirm the truth. Allowing for the changes of boy to man, the same face contrasted sharply against the chapel window.

seven

No, no, Nancy's disbelieving heart silently screamed. It couldn't be. Damon, the boy who had ripped her life to shreds? Impossible! Yet the evidence condemned, tried, and convicted him. Dr. Barton's face against the window could be no other than the face she'd seen twenty years before on that fateful night.

At first horror left her numb. All remembrance of the Sunday she had promised God she would try to forgive fled. She hastily rose, one hand over her mouth and stumbled to the side aisle, thankful no one had chosen to sit in the row.

"Nancy?" A gentle hand fell on her shoulder. A concerned voice asked, "Are you all right?"

She wanted to shriek, to cry out in the quiet chapel that her world had just ended for the second time, again because of him. She did neither. Shaking her head, she slipped from beneath his strong fingers and bolted. Could she make it to the rest room in time? Sickness rose within her and she blindly felt her way down the endless corridor, made it inside, and locked the door. There. She'd be safe. Deep breathing settled her down and her stomach stopped churning enough for her to think clearly. She must escape, now. In moments, Damon would send

Jonica Hamilton for her; she couldn't be here. The incident had wrenched open a half-closed door and brought back memories from the dim recesses of childhood. Not only of the fire, but of the terrible life afterwards.

"I can't talk about it. Not to Damon or Dr. Paul or Jonica. Not to anyone," she brokenly told the sick-looking woman in the mirror. "God, help me get out of here. Please." She straightened, unlocked the door, and made a run for it. Good, no one in sight yet. A hysterical laugh slipped from between her tightly compressed lips. She didn't even have her car. Gathering her courage, she headed down the street in search of a cab or phone booth.

Fate proved kind. A cruising cab picked her up just a block from the chapel. "Where to, ma'am?"

"Shepherd of Love Hospital." She climbed inside.

"Right."

Before they got away from downtown, Nancy had regained the ability to think clearly. Damon would immediately go to the hospital looking for her. "Driver, it's such a nice day I think I won't go home yet." She bit her lip, wishing she hadn't given away that she lived at Shepherd of Love. If Damon tried to trace her through the cab driver, the fewer clues she left, the better. Too late now. As one in a dream she heard herself giving Helen Markel's address. At the same time she felt in her purse. Her fingers tightened on the cool metal key that spelled security and a place to hide. A rush of gladness that she had never told Dr. Barton she'd taken his advice and sought counseling left her weak with relief. Someday she must face him but not until time had softened the terrible blow life had dealt in the telltale moment she had seen his face highlighted by the sun through the stained glass.

She added a generous tip when she paid her taxi driver and smiled a little at his hearty, "Thank you, ma'am!" Such a small thing to bring such a big grin. When he drove away, she had the strange feeling she'd lost a friend.

Nancy opened the door into quietness, peace, cool-ness, and a place to heal. "If I hadn't promised Helen to leave Seattle, I'd stay right here, God," she whispered. The off-white walls and pastel furniture held out loving arms of welcome. Her racing heartbeat slowed. She took off her suit jacket and hung it in a closet. Her fine eye-brows came together in a frown. It wouldn't be safe for her to risk going to her suite at the staff residence to get her packed bags and car. The smart thing was to hide out here overnight, or at least until sometime after midnight, before attempting to go back. She doubtfully peered into a mirror. Her suit skirt and shell weren't all that com-fortable to lounge in.

"Helen won't mind," she reassured herself and walked into the master bedroom. Distaste filled her at the idea of rummaging through her friend's clothing but she had no choice. A simple cotton housedress caught her atten-tion, green and white checked gingham, crisp and cool. It would do nicely and be easy to wash.

Nancy slipped into the dress. For some unknown

reason she thought of the day she had told the hospital director she didn't look well in blue or green. Her lips tightened. If the dress were yellow or even pink, she didn't know if she could have put it on.

Making sure the front door was locked, she went into the backyard and dragged a chaise lounge into the shade of a towering maple whose leaves rustled above her. She sat down, leaned back and stared at the patches of blue visible through the branches. The time had come to consider what had happened and what she should do.

"God, is it possible I'm mistaken?" Her low cry expressed her desire to believe it. She slowly shook her head. There simply was no chance of mistaken identity with the boy's features etched into her mind.

Why hadn't Damon told her? He knew her history. . . .

Nancy sat bolt upright, trying to remember every detail. So still a resident squirrel ran down a tree trunk and eyed her with a sharp gaze, she stretched her mind to remember every word she had said to him about her past. "I told him I had nightmares about death and fire," she whispered. "And that I sang to Leila, who died a long time ago. Damon was there when I asked Timmy to tell Leila I'd be coming soon to be with her. Beyond that, he knows nothing." Relief filled her. At least Damon hadn't deliberately hidden his past from her because he knew the part he had played in it.

Suddenly she regretted not wanting to know the young boy's name. At the time and through the years, she'd felt it would merely add to her burden. Now it opened a way to discover if what she had learned really concerned Dr. Barton. Police records could tell her what she passionately longed to know. If Damon had spent time in a place for juvenile offenders, there must be records.

Her heart sank. Once a minor reached eighteen, his past was officially blotted out. Her great idea dead-ended. The law forgave and allowed offenders to start over.

Forgiveness. Bittersweet memories of her experience that Sunday morning washed over her. Nancy closed her eyes, trying to retrieve the feelings so strong they had swept away long-held resentment and hatred. They wouldn't come. All she could see was the boy's face, then Damon's, against a burning background. Her heart twisted with pain. She switched mental channels. Now she saw the strong doctor who comforted Timmy and his mother; whose sad eyes with the little lines around them carved by life brightened or grew tender with compassion. What if he had made terrible mistakes as a teenager? Must he pay for it forever?

"God, I truly want to forgive him," Nancy prayed. "But could I ever forget, even if he cares as I do?" The prayer and question pounded away until she fell asleep in the chaise from pure emotional and mental exhaustion.

Nancy awakened to the evening coolness that makes Seattle delightful on most hot days. Sleepy birds sang in a low, minor key. Flowers nodded, all except the evening primroses that snapped their chalice-like blossoms open with a little pop. More refreshed than she'd have believed possible, Nancy stretched and realized hunger pangs took precedence over all else. She foraged in the immaculate kitchen and smiled at the well-stocked refrigerator. Helen obviously had suspected Nancy would come. Now the nurse opened a can of chunk chicken, boiled and cooled an egg, washed greens, chopped tomatoes and onions. The resulting chef salad plus toast with some of Helen's wonderful homemade jam did a great deal in lifting her spirits.

"Thank You, God, for this food and that I'm on vacation," she murmured. She laid her plans. Early to bed with an alarm clock set for four o'clock would give her ample time for her surreptitious visit to the residence hall. She'd be in and out before the night shift got off and the day shift rose.

&

Like a child playing hookey, she tiptoed into her rooms from her outside entrance. She'd need two trips to get her bags. Nancy hadn't realized she had been holding her breath until she closed the door behind her, felt her way to the windows to make sure the drapes were tightly closed, and let a little sigh of relief escape. She flicked a light switch—and froze.

On the living room rug just inside the door from the hall lay a square white envelope with *NANCY* written on it in bold black ink.

Damon. She'd seen his writing on too many charts to fail to recognize the penmanship. Her purse slid to the floor from weak fingers and she crossed to the envelope, eyeing it as a mouse eyes a cat ready to spring. In one quick swoop she snatched it up and ripped it open.

What is it, Nancy? she read. *Is there any way I can help? Why did you run away from the chapel? Please call me as soon as you come in, no matter how late.*

His dear and familiar scrawled signature ended the note.

Tears she had stifled all day gushed, although a tiny warm spot created by his concern glowed within her. She saw the attractive rose and white room through a waterfall, blurred and a little out of focus. Her gaze rested on the phone. If only she could call him! What release it would be to frankly tell him the entire story and ask if he were that boy.

"No." Both tears and grasping at straws left her. Until she could decide what to do and how to handle it if her worst suspicions proved accurate, she must not approach Damon.

"I'll go away as planned," she said. "The beach will give me time."

A prayer in her heart, the note in her purse, Nancy successfully made her escape without detection. Her unconquerable sense of humor arose and sustained her, fed by the picture of Nurse Galbraith sneaking out in the middle of the night, weighed down by bags. "If this is what a criminal feels like I'd never make a good one," she murmured. "I haven't done anything wrong but I feel like one pursued."

The feeling persisted all the way from Seattle to the small cabin she had rented a few miles north of Long

Beach. It evaporated when she stepped inside the furnished cabin, and fled entirely while she grocery shopped. No eating in restaurants for her unless she got sick of her own company, which wasn't likely. The solitude of the cabin suited her. So did the friendly lights a little distance away that appeared at sundown. If she needed help, she could get it. If not, no one would bother her.

At first she found it satisfying enough just to explore the beach at different hours of the morning, afternoon, and evening. She loved it best when the great red sun paused on the ocean's edge and slipped out of sight after coloring the world purple, rose, and gold. Only then did her reluctant steps turn homeward. After the first evening, she always left a light in her window. Somehow it tied her to generations of those who had wended their ways to cottage and mansion, from field or market or business—all eager for the moment they could step into a home whose lighted windows beckoned them.

Nancy nodded to grown-ups, talked with children, patted friendly dogs who came to her. Yet she held back from forming friendships. She hiked and bravely swam, but not far. The cold Pacific waters turned her blue as their depths when she stayed in too long. By the end of the week she felt the wisdom Helen Markel had used in insisting Nancy take a vacation. Her daily Bible study and prayer reinforced and strengthened her.

"Lord," she wistfully said one evening while staring into the glow of a small fire she'd built in her miniature fireplace. "Can I take this peace home? Right now I

feel I can go back to Pediatrics and do my job without it
tearing me apart when I lose a child. Please, help me to
keep close to You, for their sake—and mine." A snap-
ping stick sounded loud in the quiet room. "I have to
talk with Damon. You know this decision hasn't been
easy, but You've told us to do to others as we want them
to do to us. It's going to be hard and painful—for both
of us. Yet it's what I'd want if our roles were reversed.
I need Your help."

She sat until the fire flickered and died, not moving
until the room grew chill. Could she confront Damon?
An idea flared, along with a final, sizzling coal. *Why
not write him a letter?* The idea appealed to her. She
could start with the reason she had run from the chapel
and him. He would have time to consider the letter before they talked face-to-face.

Nancy shook her dark head. Sadness crept into her
heart. A letter would not allow either of them to see the
other's expression or to answer in person.

"Maybe it's just too soon," she told God. "So many
times in the Bible You've cautioned us to wait. Until
the time comes when I feel right about it, I won't rush
ahead."

The vow freed her and she slept dreamlessly. Yet when
Friday came, she called the travel agent and arranged to
extend her stay through Thursday of the following week.
He genially agreed; another party wanted the cabin starting Friday, if possible.

Precious day after precious day went by. Nancy alter-
nated between never wanting to leave the coast and the

stirrings inside that left her homesick for her suite in the staff residence, for Pediatrics and most of all, for a tall, handsome children's specialist who had captured her heart. On Friday morning, she left the cabin with mixed emotions, yet more confident about herself and the future than ever before in her life and closer to the God she loved and served. She resisted the temptation to go straight to the hospital and instead headed for Helen Markel's home. What luxury—another few days to make the transition from vacation back to work. She remembered Helen's comments and realized how true they were. A person really did need two weeks to get away from their routines. Nancy meant to see that in the future she took time off.

❧

Her high resolves to see Damon and tell him she needed to talk with him changed to a total fiasco. Monday morning when she reported for work, a furious, haggard doctor waylaid her before she reached the ward.

"Where have you been? Nancy Galbraith, what do you mean walking out on me and disappearing for two weeks?" he raged.

Resentment replaced the twinge of pity for his distress. "I went on vacation. Nurses do take time off," she flippantly replied, even though her heart raced like a diesel engine.

"Of all the inconsiderate. . ." He grabbed her shoulders and his expression warned he'd like to shake the living daylights out of her. "No one knew where you were. Don't you care that you've worried your friends?

Dr. Paul and Jonica and I have wracked our brains trying to figure out what sent you skylarking out of the
chapel and off to heaven knows where!"

"I'm sorry that you troubled yourself, Dr. Barton."
She became aware of a student nurse standing open-
mouthed nearby. "Now if you will remove your hands
from my shoulders, I'll get on with my work. As I'm
sure you're aware, Monday mornings are no time for
staff members to stand around airing personal griev-
ances." Her voice shook.

Damon's hands dropped. A glacial look replaced some
of the anger in his eyes. "Very well, Nurse Galbraith.
Just don't think this settles anything between us." He
executed a 180-degree about-face and marched off, in-
dignation in every line of his stiff back and head held
high.

"Welcome back to the real world," Nancy muttered.

"D-did you say something?" the student stammered.

"Nothing worth repeating." She pasted a smile on her
face to hide the ache in her heart and consoled herself by
thinking, at least he must care a little if he can get that
upset just because I take off for a time.

She made it through the day, alternating periods of
gladness by reacquainting herself with patients and fellow nurses, with an inevitable letdown. In spite of herself, her irritation grew at the highhanded way Damon
had verbally attacked her. Well, when they had their
little talk, she had some things to tell him, too. He needn't
think he could be colder than ice cubes for weeks then
turn around and expect her to report in to His Highness.

"It didn't take long to lose the peace," she ruefully admitted at the end of her shift. "Oh well, the sooner we have it out, the better."

Alas for Nancy's dream. Her telephone remained busy with all the wrong voices. Her charges exacted full measure of devotion to their needs. Dr. Barton made no move to carry out his veiled threat of a day of reckoning. A miserable week passed, then another. Doubts crept in. Nancy remembered her vow to wait for the right time. It obviously hadn't yet come. Damon barely spoke to her on the ward, although she surprised a look she couldn't define in his dark gaze several times. Her patience wore thin. So did her body. Even the excellent food Shepherd of Love served to staff and patients alike held little interest for her. In vain she chided herself as a love-sick weakling. It did little good.

With each passing day, anger smoldered. Why should Damon treat her like an outcast? She had done nothing except leave an impossible situation.

He doesn't know that, her heart reminded.

Torn with conflict, she snapped back, "He will." The postponing of the inevitable meeting in which everything must pour out left her ragged-nerved. It had been easy at the beach to visualize a rational exchange that would end with the past buried forever. Now her lips set in a straight line and her eyes flashed. How could she ever have cared for such a pigheaded, overbearing individual? She marvelled at how those traits never appeared in his dealings with others.

"Con man," she branded him, then shivered at what

she had said. If all she now felt to be true were real, Damon *had* served time.

One evening when Nancy felt she could bear the suspense no longer, she dialed Damon's home number. The phone rang. Five times. Six. Seven. At last a voice said,

"Hello." It came jerkily, as if the speaker had been running.

"Damon?"

"He isn't here." *Click*. The connection broke.

Face flaming, Nancy dropped her phone like a burning brand. How dare Dr. Damon Barton have the nerve to calmly lie to her and say he wasn't home? Fury stronger than any she had ever known set fire to her brain. She grabbed a light jacket, threw it over the uniform she hadn't bothered to change, dug car keys from her purse and headed for the door. Maybe she was running before God. Right now she didn't care. No one could insult her like this and get away with it.

She reached for the doorknob and remembered she didn't have the address. A quick check of the phone directory took care of that. She scribbled down the address and slammed the door behind her, taking pleasure in its decided thud.

"Ready or not, here I come," she gritted between clenched teeth. "You and I have a lot of talking to do; no way am I going to wait any longer. Not after this."

She climbed into her car, revved the motor, and drove out of the staff residence lot like an avenging angel bent on annihilating a foe.

eight

A faint warning bell rang deep in Nancy Galbraith's brain when she lifted her hand to knock on Dr. Damon Barton's door, a gut-level feeling of something amiss. She ignored it, an action she'd been trained not to take during her years of nurses' training.

"Come in," Damon's voice sounded strained, muffled.

She turned the knob, pushed open the door, and stepped inside. The niggling little feeling pinched at her again. Dr. Barton sat draped over a chair. The scent of tobacco tainted the air. Dim light came from a single turned-on lamp that left Damon's face in shadow.

"You could at least have the courtesy to rise," she snapped. Disillusionment ran through her like a river in flood.

"Why?" His insolence poured gasoline on the fire of her anger. She stepped away from the door, leaving it ajar. Guessing at the probable location of a wall light switch, she reached to her left.

"Don't turn on the light!" The lounging figure leaped to his feet and crossed the room in two giant steps. "Who are you and what do you want, anyway?"

Nancy slowly iced. She backed away from him flung the door wide, turned, and ran into the hall.

"Nancy, what on earth are you doing here?" a familiar voice demanded. Strong hands caught and held her shoulders in a vise-like grip. Black eyes blazed down at her.

"Damon?" She stood stock-still, trying to understand. She shook her head, closed her eyes, and looked at him again. In the subdued hall light that still outshone the feeble light streaming through the apartment door, he looked worried. "Then who—it wasn't you, after all—"

Steel undergirded his words when he said, "Come inside, Nancy." He dropped his hands but one took her arm. The touch left her weak with relief, or did it come from knowing he hadn't lied to her?

A lazy drawl from the unknown man brought her to her senses. "Well, brother, aren't you going to introduce me?" Nancy watched the man she'd mistaken for Damon in the dim light saunter back to his chair.

"How did you get in here?" A deep line cut between Damon's brows and he ignored the question.

"I have ways. Don't turn on the light," he repeated when Damon reached for the switch.

Dr. Barton smothered an exclamation, strode across the room, and pulled the drapes shut. "Are you in trouble again?"

Nancy hated the way the man who called Damon brother looked her over. She'd encountered some seamy things in her work, including men with greedy eyes. The same expression in a slightly more refined way rested on the intruder's face.

"Since my dear brother won't introduce us, I will." He stood and made a mocking bow. "I'm Curtis Barton,

Damon's older brother, and at your service. Very much at your service." He bowed low in a caricature of a knight kneeling before his lady.

"I asked why you were here," Damon's voice sliced the performance in half.

"If I had known you expected—a visitor—I wouldn't have come."

Nancy felt tarnished by her presence in the apartment, although it wasn't late. Why had she rushed here? She should have known Damon would never lie to her and hang up so rudely.

"You'll forgive my lack of manners earlier, won't you?" Curtis continued. His pretense of humility sickened her.

A strong hand shot out and grabbed his shirt front. "If you've done anything to her, you'll pay for it," Damon told him. His face set in harsh lines.

Curtis jerked free and his eyes half-closed. "I didn't touch her. She came waltzing in here, got off a bunch of stuff about my not getting up and headed out when I asked who she was."

"Is that right, Nancy?"

"Yes." She marvelled the word could get past the growing ball of disgust for herself and pity for Damon that formed in her throat.

"Did you need me?" His fierce glance softened to midnight velvet.

With all my heart, she wanted to cry out. Instead, she took a deep breath and substituted, "It's just that when I called you—Curtis—said you weren't here and I thought it was you and couldn't understand why you'd lie." She pressed her lips together and turned blindly toward the door. "I'll see you some other time, Dr. Barton." Perhaps the note of formality would remove some of the innuendo Curtis had injected into a perfectly innocent situation. She gallantly lifted her head, said, "Good night," and marched out with Damon right behind her. Not for a million dollars would she recognize the introduction or presence of Curtis with his open sneer. If she did, Nancy had the feeling Damon would give his brother a well-deserved punching out.

Damon closed the door behind them and laid a detaining hand on her sleeve. Anxiety clouded his fine eyes. "Why did you really come?"

How could she open a dialogue that reached twenty years into the past when he looked so haggard and upset? She mentally shook her head and quietly said, "Some time when it's right, we need to talk." A quick flare of agreement threatened her control when he nodded briefly, so she added, "Not now."

He walked her out to her car and she knew he watched her out of sight. Churned by emotion, she drove home in a half-daze, torn by the encounter but keeping a careful lookout for traffic lights and possible hazards. Why did the day of reckoning she knew must come loom even more ominous than before? Had the restrained violence in Damon's face when he had confronted his brother shown her a new and frightening side of the kindly doctor she'd fallen in love with, a side that could be a hangover from childhood wildness?

Nancy sighed, thinking of the sunny, halcyon days when she and Damon had shared dinners and drives. Where had they gone?

"I wish we'd never gone to the chapel," she passionately whispered. "Then I wouldn't have seen him in that stained glass light that brought everything back. Better never to have known who the boy was than this terrible fighting and ache inside."

Nancy sighed, completed her drive, and dragged into her suite of rooms. Even their quietude failed to revive her sagging spirits.

"Dear God," she prayed, on her knees just before crawling into bed. "I can't handle any of this. Please, help me. Open a way so. . ." Her voice trailed and died. For a long time she remained in the kneeling position, until a whisper of peace and God's love reminded her He understood all the things she could not say.

Five minutes after she had reached Pediatrics the next morning, a summons from the hospital director came. Wondering, she crisply instructed the other nurses to carry on, smoothed her peach uniform, glanced in a mirror to make sure every shining hair lay in place, and went to answer the call.

Nancy's heart did an involuntary little skip when a tall, handsome doctor met her just outside the director's office.

"I'm sorry about last night." He looked as if he wanted to explain but something held him back.

She shrugged. "I shouldn't have come."

"Wrong." A slow smile relaxed his tense expression. "You will always be welcome." He abruptly changed tone. "Nancy, I hope you'll consider carefully what you're going to hear."

Her eyes opened wide. *How could he know?* The wild notion this summons had something to do with the interchange in Dr. Barton's apartment crossed her mind, only to be rejected. What could an obviously hostile brother have to do with her, especially anything that affected her work?

Damon had asked himself the same question the night before. His steps had lagged on the way back to his apartment after watching Nancy out of sight. He still couldn't figure out why she had come. His pulse quickened. Would the day ever come when he could tell her of his love? His mouth twisted. Not with Curtis hanging to him like an albatross, casting a dark shadow over his life. He hadn't seen his brother since the strange encounter downtown weeks earlier. Yet here he was, parked in Damon's apartment, filling it with smoke in spite of Damon's injunction against it. Had he charmed the manager again?

"No," Curtis said when asked. "I took an impression and had a key made. Thought it might come in handy." He lit a cigarette.

"Either put that out or get out," Damon roughly told him. "Where do you get off thinking you can break in here and make yourself at home?"

Curtis squashed the barely-lighted cigarette in a cup already filled with butts. Evidently he'd been there quite some time before Nancy arrived. "Something's about to go down. I figured I'd be safe here."

"Great." Damon stared at his unwanted guest. "You get in over your head and come sneaking here looking for a hideout. Nothing doing."

"Forgotten about the slab and the morgue?" Curtis inquired. He laughed significantly when Damon winced. "How'd you like to get me out of your face for a long time? I met someone who says Vancouver, B.C. is really hopping. Maybe I'll try a new country and see if my luck changes."

For the first time Damon looked beneath the veneer of bravado and saw the change in Curtis. The expensive suit needed cleaning, the fancy shoes were scuffed, and he wore a general rundown air. "When are you going to get smart and get out of the rackets?" he demanded, hands on hips.

"I might just consider it if I had a—*friend*—like the one who just left. What did you say her name was? Oh, yeah, Nancy. Nancy what?" His eyes slitted and he cocked his head to one side. "Not bad." He laughed again, a thoroughly unpleasant sound. "Since you aren't jumping at the chance to get rid of me, I don't see why family loyalty should keep me from dating her up."

"Family loyalty!" Damon drove the nails of his clenched fists into his palms to keep from attacking his brother. "When did you ever have any? If you remember correctly, I—"

"Sure, always the hero. Not such a bad idea, actually. You're so pure I can count on any promises you make being kept," Curtis taunted.

Damon ignored the thrust. "If you ever get near Nancy with your rotten lifestyle, I'll stop you if it means turning you over to the police myself."

"You wouldn't!" Curtis flinched as if struck.

Damon's steady gaze never left his face. "You just said how well I keep my promises. Have you ever known me to break one?"

"No."

"You above all people know what giving my word means. Don't forget it."

Curtis stood. "And you won't lend me money."

"No."

Despair mingled with recklessness and desperation in his watching gaze. "Then it's off my back and your responsibility what happens."

"What's that supposed to mean?" Damon raised a skeptical eyebrow, hating the conversation but unwilling to end it until he learned more.

Curtis recaptured his strutting. "Just what I said." He stretched, yawned. "You know I can find out who Nancy is. She had on a uniform; she knows you well; calls you Dr. Barton. Easy enough matter to check the hospitals and learn her last name." His arms fell to his sides and he added, "Of course, for certain considerations. . . ." He let it hang.

"I told you what I'd do if you get near her. Neither will I be blackmailed. Now get out of here before I forget everything I believe and let you have it." Damon took a step nearer, almost hoping Curtis would make the final move and justify the licking of his life, one he should have been given years before.

"You're in love with her, aren't you. Good enough for me." He shrugged carelessly. "Plenty of women in my life already."

"Not like Nancy." Damon couldn't have held back the comment if his life had depended on it.

A strange look, so fleeting it couldn't be identified, swept over his brother's face. To Damon's amazement, Curtis made no attempt to answer. He opened the door, stepped into the hall, and glanced both ways. "Goodbye, little brother." His mocking whisper barely reached Damon's ears. The door closed behind him.

Damon crossed to the windows and opened the drapes a crack. No car purred at the apartment complex's entrance. A few minutes later he saw Curtis emerge, again look both ways, then cross the street and vanish behind a clump of bushes. His furtive movements showed his fear of being observed and Damon let the drapes swing back into place, feeling drained. A new concern piggybacked on his worries about his brother. What if Curtis in some way involved Nancy so that his sordid dealings touched her?

He licked suddenly dry lips at the horrible thought. Revenge took innocent lives here as well as elsewhere.

"She must not be touched," he vowed aloud. "But how can I prevent it? Anything Curtis wants, he breaks every rule to get." A vision of Nancy, so lovely and sweet in her work uniform came to mind. Even a hardened man like Curtis would admire her; any man would. He thought of that unexplainable look Curtis wore at the words, "Not like Nancy." Had his brother been contrasting her charm and integrity with those other women he bragged were in his life? The terrible chasm that lay between a Christian woman and those who chose Satan's way rose in Damon's consciousness. God's own Son had died for both. How did He feel when women—and men—deliberately refused Him? A great yearning for his brother's life and soul sent Damon to his knees. He stayed for a long time, unable to pray audibly. At last he stood, only to pace the apartment rug until morning, asking God how to protect Nancy from this new possible danger.

The answer didn't come until just after seven. Damon, the tormented, had showered, forced down some breakfast, and changed to Dr. Barton, physician and surgeon, when the phone rang.

"Yes? Mmmm. Right. I'll see about it immediately." He cradled the phone, filled with awe and rejoicing. Before he had cried for help, God had already put in motion forces to answer that cry. "Thank You," he breathed, snatched up his bag, and ran out with a far lighter heart than he would have dreamed possible even a few moments earlier. A quick session with the hospital director, a summons to Pediatrics that meant Nurse Galbraith would come soon, and the deep joy of accomplishment stilled Damon's tumult, at least for a time.

Once Nancy and Dr. Barton seated themselves, the hospital director went directly to his reason for her interview. "Nancy, Damon has a rather unusual request. I've thought it over and believe it might be a good thing. I'll let him explain."

Damon silently thanked God for the wise man's discretion. Without naming names or giving specifics, he had alerted the director to the fact that through a series of circumstances, the Pediatrics nurse could be in danger. It might be wise for her to get away from Shepherd of Love for a time. Now he frankly met Nancy's questioning gaze, glad for the validity of his call from Dr. Robert Cranston earlier.

"My boss called this morning. He'd just received a plea for help from one of the leading Seattle families. Their six-year-old son Eric has for some reason withdrawn into himself. He's always been a healthy child but since the death of his grandmother, Eric has had a terrible fear of anything to do with doctors or nurses or hospitals. The family has taken him to psychiatrists who say there's nothing wrong with him. To top it off, he needs to have some minor surgery, not immediately, but soon. He fell from a swing and broke a leg not long ago. It hasn't healed as straight as it should, and Dr. Cranston isn't satisfied."

Nancy sat silently, a puzzled look on her face.

Damon cleared his throat. "What Eric needs is to have a companion who can win his trust, give him confidence, and help him realize there's nothing to fear. Will you do it?"

"I? Why not a nurse from the register? I haven't had any psychological training since I graduated and got my R.N."

A quick look passed between Damon and the hospital director. The older man quietly said, "We both feel you are the very one for this job. The way you relate to children, especially those who are frightened, should be exactly what Eric needs."

"I agree." Damon tensed, knowing Nancy could not suspect his reason for wanting to get her in new surroundings for the time it took not only to help Eric, but to put her behind reach, should Curtis carry out his half-threat.

"You really want me to go?" she asked the director.

"I think it will be a fine thing for you both," he heartily agreed and again Damon felt thankful for the director's support.

"I suspect it won't be long, a week or so at the most," Damon explained. "You'll need to live in." He ignored the look of protest that crept into her eyes and blandly went on, "The Caxtons feel and Dr. Cranston agrees, Eric needs the continuity of having you in the house, a friend more than just someone who comes in. You'll be given time off, of course, but if you don't mind including the child when you go to church—there's one nearby—

or even shopping, you'll receive extra compensation."

"Doesn't the mother or father do those things?" she crisply inquired.

"The mother's a fluttery little woman who is totally useless in an emergency and Mr. Caxton isn't much better. Eric is an only child, born long after they'd given up hope for an heir. Surprisingly, he isn't spoiled. They simply can't cope with the change in their adored son." Damon laughed, a clear, ringing sound that brought smiles to the others' faces. "It's your chance to see a whole new social strata, Nancy," he teased. "The Caxtons live in a mansion, surrounded by well-guarded grounds and high walls. You can have breakfast in bed, lunch on the terrace, and you'll need dinner clothes; the Caxtons made it clear you will be treated as one of the family. I'll say this for them, they aren't the silly rich who consider those they employ inferior. They also don't isolate Eric by relegating him to the nursery for meals but keep him with them except on rare occasions when business dinners require a later evening mealtime than is good for a six-year-old." A frown crossed his forehead. "Mrs. Caxton thoughtfully sent word that any special clothing you need is to be considered part of your expenses and will be reimbursed."

"You were that sure of getting me?"

Laughter sent sparkles into his dark eyes. "I used the word *you* strictly in the generic sense, meaning whatever nurse took the job." He watched her slim, capable hands twist in her lap while she hesitated and felt a pang of compunction. "We know you hate leaving the ward and your special charges, but Nancy, this little boy needs you desperately. He needs your special compassion, your insight into why a child creates monsters that only exist in his mind. You will be truly serving one of God's children if you take on Eric Caxton's case."

"I agree, my dear." The director fitted the fingers of his left hand to those of his right. "You may also have the opportunity to drop some seeds of Christ's teachings in the Caxton home. During stressful times like these, hearts are often more open and fertile than at others."

Nancy shook her head. "I can't imagine preaching to a family of millionaires."

"Preaching, no. Living His pattern, yes." The director smiled at her. "Many of the wealthiest persons on earth are spiritually proverty-stricken. We sometimes forget that."

"I'll do my best," she said simply.

Damon turned away to hide the relief he knew must be painted all over him. Thank God, Nancy would be safe. Perhaps by the time she finished with Eric, whatever dire happening Curtis had hinted at would be over. All he could do was pray and trust God to continue to protect her.

And Curtis.

Damon gritted his teeth. His heart felt raw. No matter what Curtis had done, as he'd said, he was still Damon's brother—and a man who needed God.

nine

Nancy fell wholeheartedly, unreservedly in love five minutes after she had reached the Caxton mansion. She had driven what felt like miles, once she identified herself at the great gate that kept intruders out. The smiling guard waved her on, and Nancy remembered the twinkle in Damon's eyes when he told her this case offered the chance to experience a whole new social strata. Only in movies had she seen such opulence. The lawns and towering rhododendrons, rose arbors, and brightly blooming beds of annuals and perennials looked as if they had been clipped with manicure scissors, so even and straight, she blinked.

The house itself stood two stories high and shortened into wings and ells smothered in creeping vines and ivy. Perfection reigned inside as well as out. Floors and banister rails gleamed with polish that reflected the rich colors of fine paintings and costly tapestries. Yet Nancy didn't feel intimidated. A master decorator had skillfully made sure a feeling of warmth and welcome hung over the blended furnishings, Oriental rugs carelessly scattered, and gleaming bowls of flowers delicately scenting the rooms.

In spite of Damon's description of the Caxtons, she hadn't been able to form a clear picture. First glance confirmed his "fluttery little woman" image of Eric's mother, but the depths of love and concern in the light blue eyes and the way she took both of Nancy's hands in her own and whispered, "We're praying you can help our son" and her husband's fervent, "Amen," told more.

A six-year-old tornado whipped into the room—and captured Nancy's heart. Fire-engine red curls topped a grinning face. Gentian-blue eyes opened wide. "Hey, you're pretty!" Eric's mouth stretched into a gap-toothed grin and melted any possible awkwardness. "Mama, who is she?"

Nancy saw the slight drag of his right leg that betrayed an improper healing after the break but it didn't slow him down.

"This is N-Miss Galbraith, Eric." Mrs. Caxton put an arm around her son in the eternal gesture of mother-love. A wave of red touched her thin pale cheeks at the near slip. Damon had been adamant that Nancy not be introduced as a nurse. Neither would she wear any type of uniform. Friendship must come before trust. "She's going to be your companion for a time."

"Perhaps you'd like to show her around since she'll be living with us," Mr. Caxton quietly said. Nancy caught the slight tension in his stance that relaxed when Eric looked her over, grinned again, and said, "Sure. Wanna see the pool? I can swim. Can you?"

"I sure can. How about our going together?"

"Okay." He trotted ahead of her and Nancy made a V-for-victory sign behind her back to assure his parents so far all had gone well.

By the time the tall nurse and small boy toured the Caxton grounds and home, they had become firm friends. Eric obviously liked the responsibility of his guide duties and Nancy listened to his chatter, responding with a smile most of the time and a few quiet words or genuine admiration of his home. She also said a silent *thank you* to the Caxtons for their generosity in insisting she accept reimbursement for the two evening gowns and a few other things she needed to feel comfortable in her new, luxurious surroundings. She had refused the offer of a complete new wardrobe; the white and soft yellow chiffon dinner dresses highlighted her dark beauty but hadn't cost the earth and a few stars. A new swimsuit, shoes to match her new gowns, and her own street clothes rounded out what she would need for the short time she'd be here if all went well.

"I don't know who is whose slave," she laughingly told Damon when she reported in to him that evening after Eric had gone to bed. "I'm 'Miss Nancy' now—it sounds strange after being Nurse Nancy for so long. I suggested Eric just call me Nancy but his parents insisted on adding the Miss."

"We're all hoping it won't be long before you can tell him you're a nurse." Damon's voice came clear over the phone in Nancy's lovely suite of rooms next to Eric's. "There's a danger in letting it go too long; he could feel you tricked him."

"I'll do my best," she promised. They finished their conversation without one personal note yet Nancy felt warmed. She fell asleep as soon as her head touched the lacy pillows.

With the alertness to sounds in the night that had begun after the tragic fire so long ago, she roused from deep sleep and glanced at the digital clock. Two. She sat up and reached for a nylon robe, pulled it over her satin pajamas, and slid her feet into matching slippers. "Eric?" She stepped to the open connecting door to his room. A night light showed him tangled in his sheets, sleeping, but with tear stains on his face, innocent now of the harmless mischief that rested there during his waking hours. Before rousing him, she slipped into the adjoining bath, dampened a fluffy washcloth, and took it back to his bed.

"Wake up, dear." She gently shook him.

"Gramma?"

His sleepy whisper told her volumes. "No, dear. It's Nancy." She switched on the lamp on his nightstand.

"I-I thought Gramma had come back." He dug his fists in his eyes. "That's dumb, isn't it?"

Praying for wisdom, Nancy gently took his hands down and bathed his hot face. "I don't think so. After my little sister died I used to think I heard her calling." She had to swallow hard to prevent her own emotions from clouding his need.

"Really?" His eyes looked like glistening blue jewels under water and he crept closer to her.

"Really. The nurses in the hospital helped—"

His little figure stiffened. "I hate nurses and doctors and hospitals. They killed my Gramma." His face screwed into an ugly frown.

She rejoiced at learning the root of his problem so soon and at the trust he showed in telling her something she realized he must have held back in his psychiatric interviews. "I'm sorry you feel that way, Eric," she talked to him as she would to an adult. "If it hadn't been for the doctors and nurses and the hospital, I don't know what I'd have done."

She sensed a waiting, a suspended judgment in his stillness. "I was burned in a bad fire." She took a deep breath. "Tomorrow when we go swimming you'll see some lines on my back and shoulders, Eric. They would be ugly scars if doctors hadn't taken such good care of me."

"I wish Gramma had those doctors," he muttered. "They wouldn't have made her die." Eric buried his face in Nancy's lap. She felt his hot tears soaking her hand and impulsively pulled him into her arms, crooning and rocking him back and forth.

When he quieted, she asked, "Why do you think they made your Gramma die?"

A negative headshake told her nothing. Then a small voice said, "I heard Daddy and Mama talking. Mama said they never should have let Gramma go to the hospital."

"Did you ever tell anyone what you heard?"

Another headshake. "I was scared. And when I fell out of the swing and broke my leg I screamed and screamed so they wouldn't take me to the hospital. I knew I wouldn't come back."

"But you did go and you did come back," she gently

reminded.

"That's 'cause I made Mama stay with me all the time," he croaked, hoarse from crying. "Daddy says I have to go back and get my leg fixed better but I won't." His voice rose sharply. "I won't, I won't, I won't!"

"Shhh, Eric." She held him close until worn out with his fears of past and future, he fell into a troubled sleep. Nancy didn't leave him until his even breathing told her the loss of consciousness had relaxed his tired body and mind. She straightened his bedclothes and wearily slipped back to her own room. How would he greet her in the morning? Some children felt ashamed at having broken down.

"God," she prayed, eyes closed. "Please bless this hurting little boy and his family. Please give me the right words to say to all of them. In Jesus' name, Amen." She fell asleep with the same prayer echoing and re-echoing in her heart.

Nancy sensed Eric's quick glance at her when she went into his room the next morning. She had deliberately waited until she knew from the sound of his movements he'd dressed himself.

"Need help tying your shoes?" she called from the doorway.

"Naw." His gap-tooth grin opened up. A look of relief spread over his face. "D'you?"

"Naw." She imitated him and laughed at the delight dancing in his eyes. "I don't have laces. See?" She held out her right foot, clad in a low-heeled white pump.

He giggled and told her, "C'mon. Since you're dressed

you don't get breakfast in bed." He took her by one hand. "I'm hungry. Are you?"

"I'm abostively, posolutely starvationed," she solemnly replied.

"You're funny. I like you." He dropped her hand when they came to the top of the stairs leading downward. "Can you do this?" *Swish. Thump.* He slid down the banister rail and landed on both feet at the bottom.

Did she dare? Why not? Anything that brought Eric closer to his undercover nurse meant a step closer to his mental healing. She gathered the soft pink folds of her cotton dress around her, mounted the rail, and *whooshed* down.

"Perfect landing," an amused voice commented from an arched doorway nearby.

Nancy felt like a fool when she whipped around and saw Dr. Barton leaning against the side of the arch.

"Who're you?" Eric demanded, feet planted a foot apart and hands on his hips. His red curls shone in the sunlight and his lower lip stuck out.

Nancy smothered a pleased smile. So she had a new champion.

Damon grinned easily. "I'm Damon, a friend of Nancy's. I came to invite both of you to have breakfast with me and go to the Woodland Park Zoo. Anyone here want to do that?"

Eric's belligerence fled. "Me, me, me." He danced over to the visitor, grabbed both strong hands, and swung back and forth.

"Me, too, if it's all right with the Caxtons," Nancy

ungrammatically agreed.

"Why don't you have breakfast here before you go?" Mrs. Caxton and her husband came down the staircase.

"Aw, Mom, I wanta go to McDonald's," Eric complained.

"Even though the cook made cinnamon rolls for breakfast?" Mr. Caxton tempted.

Nancy saw the struggle going on inside the little boy and blessed Damon for his insight when he offered, "Why not have breakfast here—we wouldn't want to hurt your cook's feelings by not eating those cinnamon rolls, would we—then we can have lunch at McDonald's."

"All right!" Eric's world turned right-side up again. His enchanting grin flashed and he tore ahead in the direction Nancy knew from her tour the night before led to the dining room.

"We thought it might be a good idea for Eric to get to know Dr. Barton," Mrs. Caxton murmured, pausing for a moment before following her excited son. "Dr. Cranston says Dr. Barton will be doing the corrective surgery."

Again Nancy had the feeling of unplumbed depths in her hostess. It gave her food for thought that accompanied the delicious rolls, freshly squeezed orange juice, crisp bacon, and iced melon.

"Hurry, Miss Nancy," Eric prodded. "I'm through already." He swiped his napkin across his mouth and bounced on his chair.

"Go brush your teeth, dear." His mother smiled at him and a mist rose to the nurse's eyes. How like her own mother it sounded, when she had reminded her girls so long ago.

"Are your shoes good for walking?" Damon asked. "There's a lot of ground to cover at the Zoo."

"I think I'll change to tennis shoes," Nancy told him.

Surely sometime during the day she would have the chance to quiz Damon about the fire. The thought depressed her but she shoved it aside. If her suspicions were accurate, this might be the last day she and Damon would spend together. *Then let it be perfect*, she told herself. *Don't let anything spoil it.*

Nancy hadn't counted on Eric's boundless energy when she planned for a quiet time with Dr. Barton. One hand in each of theirs, he dashed here and there, pulling them along. At times he jerked free and ran ahead. "I haven't been here since I was a little kid," he told them. He didn't notice how Damon covered his mouth and Nancy turned away to hide her smile. Every new sight brought him closer to the adults. His high laugh made heads turn and brought a look of joyous understanding to those around him, as well.

What if she and Damon were married and had a little boy like Eric, Nancy wondered. Of course he wouldn't have red hair or blue eyes, but the velvet dark eyes of the imaginary child would hold the same wonder; his laugh would ring sweet and clear, just as Eric's did. *Please, God, I just have to talk with Damon*, Nancy wordlessly prayed.

Yet the day sped by on flying feet. McDonald's beckoned. The afternoon passed and when Damon drove

Nancy and her charge to the Caxtons', Eric contentedly leaned against her arm. "This is the bestest day ever," he mumbled, "'cept my old leg hurts—just a little," he hastily added, obviously loath to complain in case it meant missing out on future fun.

"When you get it fixed, we'll do some other neat stuff," Damon told him. Before Eric could pop up and deny all intentions of ever going to a hospital again, Dr. Barton went right on. "It takes good legs to play ball at the beach and chase chipmunks at Mount Rainier."

Eric said nothing—then. Not until Nancy tucked him in and told him a story did he obliquely refer to their middle-of-the-night conversation. "S'pose the doctors who fixed you could make my leg better?"

"Oh, there are hundreds of good doctors," Nancy breezily told him. "Good nurses, too, and hospitals." She felt the familiar stiffening of his body and quickly said, "Do you mind if I say my prayers with you? It's always nicer with someone else."

Eric relaxed and sagged against her arm. "How come God can hear everybody at once?"

"Because He's God." She hugged the little boy. "You know how your daddy's computer takes in all kinds of information? Well, God is stronger and smarter than all the computers."

"Then how come He let Gramma die? I told Him not to." The age-old question from the childish lips brought an ache to Nancy's heart.

"Your mama told me your grandma had been really sick. You didn't want her to keep being sick, did you?"

"No." A violent headshake.

"Neither did God." She smoothed the tousled red curls. "It's hard to understand but God loves each of us so much sometimes He does things we don't like but what is best for those we care about."

"Like your sister?"

"Yes." She thought back weeks to another child whose fear of death needed addressing. "Just maybe your grandma and my sister are keeping each other company."

He lay so quiet against her, Nancy wondered if he'd fallen asleep. "Miss Nancy, if Gramma had stayed here with me, would she still be dead now?" He tensed.

"Yes, Eric. Her body was too sick to get well." She realized the question behind his spoken question. "The reason your mama said what she did wasn't because having your grandma stay here would have changed things, or that the hospital and nurses and doctors are bad. She knew it wouldn't have made any difference. I believe she just wished she could have kept your grandma a little longer."

"Me, too." The voice dropped to a whisper. "Will I see my gramma again? Will you see your sister?"

"Oh, yes." She hugged him. "That's the most wonderful part of God's plan. If we love Him and serve Him and ask His Son Jesus to live in our hearts, God promises that someday we will be together again. There won't be any sad times or sickness or goodbyes. Everyone in heaven will be happy and well."

"Then...I...want...to...." Eric fell asleep before he could finish his sentence. Nancy gently laid him back on his pillows, humbled by the responsibility of those who chose nursing. Body, mind, spirit, and soul all needed loving care. Again she thanked God for her profession.

The next day cemented Nancy's and Eric's friendship even more. They swam in the pool in the morning, his eyes frankly curious when she showed him the faint scars, all that remained of her burns.

"They don't show much," he told her, then patted her arm. "I'm glad the doctors fixed you."

She hesitated. Words trembled on her lips, needing to be spoken but held back in case Eric wasn't ready for them.

He wasn't, in the bright sunlight. "C'mon," he jumped into the pool, attention turned away from doctors and hospitals and nurses and fear. But that night, in the dim light of his room he asked, "If I-I get my leg fixed, will you be there?"

Her heart leaped with excitement. "I'll do better than that. If you decide to get your leg fixed, I'll take care of you afterwards."

"Promise?"

"Cross my heart." She shook hands on their pact.

His bright mind seized on a new thought that tumbled out, "What do you do when you aren't here with us? I mean, before you came to live with Mama and Daddy and me?"

With a quick prayer that his trust would stand the truth, Nancy told him, "I take care of little boys and girls like you, only usually they're sick or have had an operation."

He jerked free, sat up straight, and stared at her. "Are you a *nurse*?" Disbelief underlined each word.

"Yes, Eric. God has called me to take care of His children. He trusts me to do everything I can to help make them well. I love the children I care for, just as I've learned to love you."

He fell back on his pillows. "A nurse. But I'm not scared of you!"

"I'm not scared of you, either," she teased. Her training told her the light touch often made the necessary difference.

"You better be. I'm a tiger and if you don't be good I'll eat you up." He growled low in his throat. "Grrrr. I'm Errrrric the Tigerrrr." With the ability of children to change from serious to fantasy he threw aside everything except his growling.

"Okay, Eric the Tiger, I'll be good, good, good." She half-sang the words. "How about a *good*night hug? It's been a long day and tomorrow we're going to the beach. Right?"

"Right, Miss—uh—" He paused and his forehead wrinkled. "Are you still Miss Nancy?"

"Of course, except my patients call me Nurse Nancy. I have one little girl who has lost some front teeth and she calls me 'Nurth Nanthy'." She tucked him in again. "Goodnight, Mr. Tiger."

"Goodnight, Nurth Nanthy," he mimicked. "You won't forget?"

She almost made the fatal mistake of saying, "Forget what?" then she remembered her promise. "Nurse Nancy never forgets. When Mr. Tiger gets the knot taken out of his tail—oh, excuse me—the kink out of his leg, I'll be right there."

"Will Jesus be there, too?" The sleepy voice demanded.

Nancy blinked back tears. "I know a wonderful children's specialist who asks God and Jesus to be with him every time he operates."

Eric's eyelids drooped. He started to say something but fell asleep before words came out. Nancy knelt beside his bed, as she had done countless times before with children from every kind of home, thanking God for His goodness and asking Him to be with her patients. Tonight she added a special thanks for His calming Eric's fears.

A slight rustling sound from the doorway brought her to her feet. The Caxtons stood there, hands clasped, tears on both faces. They beckoned her into the hall and closed Eric's door behind him. "Nurse Galbraith," Mr. Caxton said. "Is the specialist you spoke of Dr. Barton?" She nodded and he continued, "My wife and I can never thank you enough for what you've done."

"It's our Heavenly Father you should thank," she told him simply.

"We already have," Mrs. Caxton put in without a trace of her usual flutter. Nancy had a feeling more had been resolved in the parents' lives even than in their child's.

ten

Long before Eric awakened the next morning, Nancy jubilantly reported the little boy's wavering fears about medical personnel and hospitals.

"Good for you," Damon told her, voice ringing through the phone. "Use your own judgment in telling him I'm a doctor, the doctor who will operate on his leg." When she didn't answer, he sharply asked, "Or do you think I should?"

Nancy thought quickly, "I believe it might be well for us to both be there." They set up a time when Damon could get there between appointments and alerted the Caxtons what they intended to do. If Eric suspected anything when his new friend appeared for lunch, it didn't show.

Afterwards his mother said, "Dear, we want to talk to you."

"'Bout my leg?" He bit into a sandwich, washed it down with a big swallow of milk, and looked up from above a white mustache. "Nurse Nancy's gonna take care of it."

"How would you like me to fix that leg so we can do all those things we discussed?" Damon asked him.

Eric's eyes looked like sapphires in his face. "But you—are you a-a doctor?" A succession of expressions

131

played tag across his face; doubt, disbelief, a little remaining fear. The next instant his smile reappeared.
"Hey, are you the guy Nurse Nancy told me about last
night? The one who asks God and Jesus to help you do
what you're s'posed to?" he interrogated.

"I certainly am," Damon told him. "Why, I'd no more
try and fix a leg or anything else without having God's
help than you'd wave your arms and fly up to the ceiling!"

"Well," Eric said when he stopped laughing. "You
can fix my leg if God and Jesus and Nurse Nancy's
there."

"Deal." Damon shook with his brand new patient.

"You gonna do it today?" Eric demanded.

"It will take a few days to get things set up," Nancy
told him. An idea struck her. "How would you like to
go with me to the hospital and see the place you'll be?
I'm sure we will want to keep you for a little while.
Besides, my other patients are probably missing me. This
will give you a chance to get acquainted and I can check
on them."

"Sure." Eric finished his milk and beamed. "Let's go."

Nancy told him on the way to Shepherd of Love, "Everyone here asks God to help them, and we're trying to
make a lot of people well." She explained that they must
be very quiet in the halls; she had special permission to
let him visit. Dr. Barton and the Caxtons trailed along
behind the other two.

When they reached the ward with its bright colors, a
chorus of, "Nurse Nancy! We missed you," greeted them.

Eric clung to her, palm moist until a boy a little older

who had his leg in a cast hollered, "Are you gonna be here? What for? I got a broken leg."

"Mine got broken, too," Eric said. "But it didn't get fixed right, so Dr. Barton's gonna make it do what it's s'posed to."

"He's neat," the older boy said. "He fixed my leg." He wiggled his toes, bare beyond the cast. "You get treated good here. Nurse Nancy's super and the food . . .mmmm." Before they left, he and Eric had formed the beginnings of friendship.

At the Caxton's request, Nancy remained in their home for the short time it took to schedule Eric's surgery. He came through beautifully and his new friend was right there in the ward to greet him. Damon and Nancy had encouraged Eric's parents to let him stay a few days beyond the minimum, then Nancy would go home with him for another week. She found herself wet-eyed the day she finally left, knowing as long as she lived, the Caxton home would be open to her. She also hugged a wonderful secret. Mrs. Caxton had shared that she and her husband planned to adopt a child as near Eric's age as possible just as soon as they could find one and be approved. "We also plan to start setting some priorities and number one is to start giving something back to God for all He's done," she added. "Not just financially. My husband and I are talking about possibly volunteering somewhere we are really needed." New interest sparked in her eyes. "Perhaps at the wonderful Christian school we found for Eric. Or helping tutor those who are illiterate."

"Seattle has many needy in many ways," Nancy soberly said. "I know whatever you choose to do will be valuable."

Eric scrubbed at his eyes when he said good-bye then gave her what he called a "tiger hug" with both arms tight around her neck. "You won't forget me?" he pleaded.

"Not if I live to be twice as old as Methuselah," she promised. Nancy had been reading Bible stories to him while he recuperated, and Eric always laughed at the picture in his storybook of the old, old man.

"That's a long time," Eric said. "Good-bye, Nurse Nancy." He cocked his head to one side and gave her his best grin. "Tell my friends at the Ped-yat-rix hi and come see me. 'Member, I'm Errrric the Tigerrrr. You gotta be good or I'll come eat you up."

She left with the drop of sadness that always filled her overflowing cup of gratitude when a child no longer needed her. Perhaps by the next time she saw Eric, he'd have a sister or brother. "It's so hard knowing I won't mean as much to them," she brokenly whispered. "God, someday, I want children I won't have to tell good-bye until they're grown."

One thing cheered her. Damon had asked her to reserve the evening for him. By the time she got resettled into her suite, showered and dressed, he'd be there to pick her up. She went from warm to cold and back again. She could not put off telling Damon why she had run out of the chapel that Sunday morning several weeks before.

The leaves of autumn had replaced some of summer's

glow. The smell of wood fires from homes that had no other means of heating put a tang in the air. Crisp nights and early morning gave way to sunny but subdued afternoons. Heavy dew sparkled and grass lay wet underfoot when she stepped outside.

Nancy held her breath when she walked into her apartment, half afraid her stay with the Caxtons might have spoiled her for her more modest surroundings. It hadn't. The rose and white had retained their charm and even the lack of spaciousness to which she'd grown accustomed couldn't dim the feeling of coming home.

She dressed for her date with exceptional care. Once before she had felt it would be her last time with Damon; Eric's glee at the zoo had eliminated any chance of private conversation with him. Tonight nothing must stand in the way. Her hands trembled and she had to try twice to apply the touch of lipstick she wore. Unable to decide if she faced Paradise or the guillotine, she steadied herself with the deep breathing that always helped, and answered the firm knock at her door.

Damon had never looked more handsome than when she opened the door and he smiled at her. A pang shot through her. Why, of all the men on earth, did he have to be the one she'd learned to love? On the other hand, how could she even think of loving another? The mental questions kept her busy trying to concentrate on his hospital chitchat on the way to the restaurant that overlooked Puget Sound. He had reserved a quiet window table that offered a measure of privacy. Fresh flowers adorned the white tablecloth. Soft background music enhanced the atmosphere rather than overwhelmed patrons.

Somehow she managed to keep things light during the excellent meal: steak for him, delicious prawns for her, with the crispest of salads, baked potatoes bursting with goodness, and raspberry sorbet after the meal. Several times Nancy glanced out the window at the massed gray clouds over the Sound. Although the double glass drowned the cries of the seagulls winging in the dusk, she felt the sadness of a fall evening. Soon Daylight Savings Time would end and darkness would come even earlier. Nancy shivered in spite of the restaurant's warmth. The dying day had lowered her spirits. Dread of what lay just ahead filled her.

"Nancy, there's something wrong between us. What is it?" Sharp as a surgeon's scalpel his question cut through her depression.

"I. . .we have to talk."

His warm hand covered hers where it rested on the white cloth. The expression in his eyes set her heart to pounding and regret rose to choke her. "Where would you like to go?" He paused. "I can't invite you to my apartment. Curtis has a way of popping in at unexpected and inconvenient times."

She thought of the living room at the staff residence building and shook her head. No, too much chance of interruption. Ditto for her small suite. The vision of off-white walls and pastel furniture hovered in her mind. "We can go to Helen Markel's. Her California friends insisted she stay a lot longer than she had planned. She also met someone who needed her and you know what that means to her!"

"I certainly do." After he paid their bill and they got back in his car he casually added, "I didn't know you were acquainted with Helen."

She remembered she had never told him of her counseling sessions and quickly said, "Oh, yes. She's a darling, isn't she?" Their discussion of the valiant lady lasted all the way to the welcoming home and until Nancy seated herself in a comfortable chair with Damon across from her.

"Well, Nurse Nancy?" The light tone belied the concern she saw shining in his dark eyes. "It goes back to the Sunday at the chapel, doesn't it?"

She shot a prayer for help skyward and laced her fingers in her lap. "No, Damon. It goes back a lot farther." She looked at him, pleading for help. His quiet demeanor steadied her, although she sensed a tension in him like a mountain lion preparing to spring.

"You know I lost a sister a long time ago," she began. "It nearly destroyed me. Not the burns I received in the fire, but the searing memories." Gaze firmly fixed on her hands, she felt rather than saw his involuntary start. She hurried on, knowing if she hesitated she would never dredge up the past, no matter how vitally important it was to do so. In a monotone voice, to keep from breaking down, she relived for him how she had awakened coughing, a frightened four-year-old taught to instantly obey her mama. She described the flames, her mother's command to run, Leila's outstretched arms, the pain across her shoulders. Tears dripped onto her clenched hands when she breathlessly said, "The house crashed and roared. I watched my home with Mama and Leila collapse. Then. . ." Her voice failed her.

"Nancy, darling, don't go on!" Strong arms reached and held her. She had the feeling as long as she stayed where she was nothing on earth could ever again hurt her. Lips dry, she forced herself back from Damon's comfort. *She must continue.*

"Please. There's more." She heard his quick prayer, "Dear God!" but steeled herself against it. "Just before I fainted I saw a dark figure." She closed her eyes then opened them and risked a glance at Damon. He sat stony-faced as Mount Rainier when the snow melted and left sheer rock exposed to view. In all her work, Nancy had never seen such agony on a human face. She looked away and went on.

"Against the flickering flames, he stood out. A boy, dark-haired, frightened-looking. I've never forgotten."

An audible gasp told her Damon's suspicions roused earlier in the story had become fact. In a fluid motion he stood, then knelt before her.

"No! I have to finish." Fingers twisted, stomach cramped from tension, Nancy refused to look at the kneeling figure, so close, yet with a chasm between. "That Sunday at the chapel, the sunlight came through the stained glass window. It backlighted your face. Oh, God." Her control broke on the prayer. "Why did I have to see you—like that?" She quivered like a cottonwood leaf, waiting, hoping he would take her in his arms and tell her she'd been mistaken, that no matter how accusing the evidence was, he hadn't set the fire.

"Then you believe I killed your family."

She looked at him then and saw the haggard expression. He'd aged ten years in the few minutes it had taken to tell her tragic story.

"I don't want to believe it," she brokenly told him.

Hope flared in his eyes, then died. So did Nancy's last shred of wishing the nightmare had ended. He didn't touch her and she felt glad. "Later, after I started to heal, the police came. They didn't wear uniforms; I've always been thankful for that. I doubt if I even knew they were policemen at the time. Anyway, they showed me pictures. I picked out the face of the boy I had seen at the fire. Sometime later I heard he had been sent to a correctional facility." She mustered her final ounce of courage and whispered, "Damon, was it you?" She searched his face, desperately hoping he would deny it.

"I served time for the setting of the fire."

Nancy shrank from the truth, bald and ugly on his lips. Yet her fascinated gaze never left his face.

"Yes, I served time. But I never committed arson," he quietly told her. A little muscle twitched in his cheek; his face remained somber.

"Then it was all an accident, a teenage prank." Her flat voice inched out from behind the world of crushed dreams in her heart.

"I can't explain. Darling, it's asking more than any woman should be expected to give, but can you trust me enough to believe I am innocent?"

"How—why—Damon, I want to believe you." She

barely noticed he had called her darling for the second time. "How can I? I *saw* you. I identified you. Now you say you're innocent." She unclenched her aching fingers and spread her hands helplessly, torn between memories and the longing to trust him.

"If only I could tell you," he cried.

"Why can't you?" she demanded. A wave of love and the desire to protect and bring him healing assaulted her.

"The awful thing is, I cannot even explain why." He rose, walked away from her, and stood staring at a picture on the wall. She could see his shoulders shake from a powerful, unidentified emotion she sensed had nothing to do with her. He wheeled back toward her, his face gray ashes. "I'll take you home."

Stunned by the suddenness of his defeat, Nancy could not protest, even though the whole disjointed conversation beat on her soul like hammers on an anvil. She silently preceded him out the door, waited while he switched off the lights and locked up, then stepped into the car when he held the door for her.

Lights from a car parked a little way behind them flashed. In their light she saw the deep sadness in Damon's weary face. She wanted to put her hand over his on the wheel, but clasped her hands instead. Before they rounded the first corner, she glanced back. Helen's home lay serene, brightened by a nearby streetlight. Would she ever again feel the peace it offered? Or would she always associate the former haven with the raw and horrible feelings she'd experienced there tonight?

She fumbled for a tissue in her purse and wiped her

eyes. The next moment Damon's voice, sharpened into command, stopped her hand midway back to her purse. "Don't panic, but I have a feeling we're being followed."

She gasped and automatically started to look behind them.

"Don't look back. I'm going to see if I can outmaneuver the driver." She saw the vertical lines form between his brows when he increased speed, cut a corner, sped another block, and turned again. The lights behind them faithfully followed.

"Who is it?"

"Probably some friends of my dear brother." He shut his lips hard and Nancy knew he would say no more. After several unsuccessful tries to ditch the car behind them, a blessed yellow light let them through and mercifully changed to red. The other car slammed to a stop then turned right before traffic from the other direction could get going.

"Now's our chance." Damon grimly speeded up.

"Can we outrun whoever it is?" Nancy inquired.

"I doubt it. Instead, we'll do something else." He slowed. Nancy saw him glance in the rear view mirror and quickly looked back. No lights. Damon heaved a sigh of obvious relief, swung into a nearby driveway, killed the motor, and shut off the lights. "Get down," he ordered. Nancy crouched forward. Damon leaned sideways in the seat. His head brushed her skirt and she blindly groped for the comfort of his hand. His fingers tightened over hers and strength flowed through her. Whatever he had been in the past, Dr. Damon Barton would guard her with his life. She shuddered. Where had that horrible thought come from? A speeding car thundered past, screeched its brakes, and tore across an intersection.

"Stay down," Damon warned. "He. . .they may come back." His admonition came none too soon. Less than a minute later the terrifying sound of a car driven by some kind of maniac bent on who-knew-what reached her ears. She crouched lower. Damon's fingers tightened. An eternity later he cautiously raised his head.

"It's all right now." He straightened, put the car in gear, and backed into the street, after freeing her hand.

"Damon, is Curtis in trouble?" she whispered, still frightened from the strange incident.

"Yes. I don't know what, this time." In the dim light his face looked lumpy. "He has a talent for getting into unpleasant situations. Until now, they—usually— haven't involved me." A forlorn note in his voice caught at her heartstrings. He sounded so like a small boy needing reassurance and unable to ask for it.

"I'll pray for him," she said.

"Thank you, Nancy." He slid his hand from the wheel long enough for a quick grip. "It's all anyone can do." The hopelessness in his words showed how much he cared. Before she could respond, he added in a far-from-casual tone, "If you don't mind, I'll swing by my apartment for just a moment before I take you home."

Her analytical mind screamed, *he doesn't want to endanger you, just in case the tail picks you up again.*

She managed to say, "All right" even though fear prickled her skin. Nancy felt her muscles knot when they turned down the street toward the apartment. A block before they arrived he saw it—a parked car, unlighted, but with motor running.

"They're here." Damon took the corner at a sedate, unsuspicious pace. Evidently the watchers didn't notice; perhaps they had counted on their quarry not expecting a tail at the apartment. Nancy peered out the window just before they got around the corner. The menacing car remained in its place just back of the entrance.

Caught in the web of intrigue surrounding them, Nancy didn't notice their route for several blocks. Then she exclaimed, "Why, this isn't the way to Shepherd of Love!"

"You aren't going back there tonight," Damon told her. "I doubt that whoever stalked us knows about you but it's impossible to be sure. The Caxtons will be happy to have you as a guest for a few more days, I'm sure."

"What about you?"

"I'm going to get to the bottom of this mess as soon as I can get my hand on Curtis." His set jaw boded no good for his brother.

"You'll be careful?" This time her hand moved of its own volition and rested on his.

"Yes, but it's time to clear up a whole lot of things."

She shivered in the warm car, wondering if her world would ever stop its topsy-turvy turning and let her and Damon get on with their lives. Even if those lives could never be joined because of what had happened in the past, this new fear for his safety made other things pale by comparison.

eleven

The Caxtons showed surprise at their unexpected visitors but when Damon explained, "For some reason we were followed tonight and until I find out why, I'd just as soon have Nancy away from the hospital," they asked no questions and invited her to stay as long as necessary.

"Eric's asleep but how thrilled he will be to wake up and find his beloved Nurse Nancy here," Mrs. Caxton told them. "We also have some great news. Just this afternoon we got a call, and it looks like some red tape will be cut. We may get a sister for Eric very soon, at least on the mandatory trial basis before adoption becomes final."

"That's wonderful! What does Eric think?"

"I'll let him tell you that for himself." A ripple of laughter warmed Mrs. Caxton's face and her husband wore a broad grin.

"Dr. Barton, why don't you stay with us, too? You know we have plenty of room and would love to have you."

Nancy knew how genuine his sigh was, how regretful his "thanks, but no thanks." He added, "I have things to straighten out."

Nancy walked with him to the door. She repeated, "Be

careful," and knew her love must shine through her eyes.

Damon rested both hands on her shoulders and looked deep into her heart. "Trust me, Nancy." The next moment he had gone, leaving her feeling more like a wishbone than ever.

The Caxtons tactfully had remained in the living room talking while Nancy speeded the parting guest. Now she took time to lean against the closed door until she could control herself.

Less than an hour later she again occupied the lovely guest suite next to Eric's rooms. Her hostess had provided gown, robe, slippers.

"There's a new toothbrush in your bathroom," she said, "as well as toothpaste, deodorant, everything you'll need. We haven't replaced you. We never will, in our hearts."

Nancy had to keep her eyes wide open to stop the tears from spilling out and distressing the woman she had come to love.

Her bedside phone rang. She eyed it the way she would a deadly snake if it had appeared on her dressing table before she picked up the receiver.

"Hello?"

"All clear," Damon's voice came. "I called the hospital director and explained you'll be gone for a little longer."

"Was the car still there?" She clutched the phone with sweaty fingers.

"No." He sounded guarded.

"Is Curtis there?"

"Not now. Good night." The phone clicked. A moment later the dial tone rang in her ear.

"Good night, Damon," she whispered into the dead phone, then cradled it. A million questions cascaded through her brain, but she found herself too tired to consider any of them. They'd still be around to bombard her tomorrow. Tonight she was safe, secure, and in no condition to even think.

"Nancy?" A light tap at her hall door brought her alive. "Come in."

Mrs. Caxton entered, holding a tumbler. "Warm milk. Just what the doctor ordered." She smiled and handed it to her guest.

Nancy obediently drank it and watched through a haze as her hostess left. *Just what the doctor ordered.* There must have been a mild sedative in the milk. She felt herself floating with dark eyes shining at her, a quiet voice repeating again and again, "Trust me." . . . .*Trust me. How could two words hold a universe of impossibility?*

❧

Damon's fine hands tightened on the wheel of his car. No man in his right mind could expect anyone to have that kind of faith when his only flimsy defense was a claim of innocence. Weighed against the skyscraper of evidence, especially Nancy's clear memory, how could it stand? Again his jaw set. The day of reckoning with Curtis would be postponed no longer.

"God, it's long past time," he prayed. "I don't want to completely alienate him or I'll never be able to bring him to You, but things can't go on like this. Tonight Nancy and I faced real danger. I could smell it. Please, help me. First of all, I have to find Curtis."

When he got to the apartment complex, Damon checked out the atmosphere. Not a glimmer of light came from his window. No car sat waiting by the curb. Still cautious, he drove to the back parking lot, into a stall marked *visitor* and locked the car behind him, a gesture he recognized as useless. The caduceus symbol told the world a doctor owned the vehicle, normally a boon, to-night a curse. He shrugged. God could protect him just as well against gang members, if that's what they were, as in his own bed. Still, he used care in going upstairs. His key sounded loud in the lock and before he stepped inside the room, he gave it a shove open and ducked to one side.

"You act like the devil himself is after you," Curtis observed from the couch. Damon hadn't realized the extent of his tension until it washed from his body. "He is. Was."

"And that means what?" Curtis turned rigid. His eyes narrowed to mere slits and he licked his lips.

"Tonight someone trailed Nancy and me. He or they must have picked me up here, followed when I went for her, waited outside the restaurant, and trailed us to—a private home." He bit back Helen Markel's name. "What are you doing, Curtis, using me for a decoy? It's you they're after, isn't it? Are you counting on our looking enough alike at a distance for whatever rats are after you to come for me?"

Curtis swore and leaped up so fast he looked like a man on a trampoline. "What exactly happened?"

"Nothing, except it scared Nancy and didn't make me happy." He scornfully related how they'd escaped. "I don't know what would have happened if they'd caught us. Do you?"

"I'm afraid to even consider it." Curtis sank back to the couch. "I never meant to get you in it."

"Then why did you?" Damon flung on his way to the bedroom. He showered, and threw on a lounge coat. The upcoming session would be long and painful. He might as well start out physically comfortable.

Curtis looked wary when his brother came back to the living room.

"All right, what is it?" Damon's heart pounded at the desperation in his brother's face.

"Revenge. From the California deal."

"I thought so. What are you going to do?"

"I don't know." His shoulders slumped. "Running didn't work."

"And in the meantime I'm a sitting duck, as well as anyone who happens to be with me."

Curtis shriveled, bravado gone. "I'm scared."

"You should be."

"Don't preach." But the old domineering older-brother sneer was missing. "What can I do?"

Naked fear shone in the dark eyes that should have held compassion. Damon took a long, unsteady breath.

"You can release me from a promise I never should have made."

In a twinkling an ugly devil-mask fell over his brother's features. "Why should I?" He leaned forward.

"Because the woman and child who died in the fire were Nancy's mother and sister." Damon let him have it full blast. Curtis just stared at him.

"I'm in love with Nancy. She's the only woman I've ever wanted or ever will. I believe she loves me. She also knows I did time in juvenile detention for arson— and that arson scarred her in a whole lot more ways than physically." Damon felt he pleaded not only for his love and Nancy's but for his brother's soul. If Curtis had any remaining decency he would say the word to end the twenty-year nightmare in which Damon had lived.

"If she doesn't believe you, why would she believe me?" Some of the sneer had returned.

"You know I haven't told her." Damon clenched his hands into fists to keep from slamming them into Curtis' face.

"You must have told her something."

"Just that even though I paid for it, I didn't set the fire."

Curtis silently eyed him for a minute before commenting, "If she's in love with you, why isn't it enough? Why's she so hot for the idea you did it?"

Damon's words fell cold and hard as pearls from a broken string to a polished, hardwood floor. "She saw a boy running. The flames behind him made an orange curtain. Later she identified the face. After struggling against her own burned shoulders and back. After continuing nightmares of her mother ordering her to run. After having the memory of her four-year-old sister holding out her hands, imploring Nancy to save her."

"Dear God!" This time Curtis' response was not blasphemy. He raised a shaking hand, wiped sweat from his forehead.

"If it hadn't been for God, she wouldn't have survived. She did. She became a Pediatrics nurse because of Leila, reasoning that she'd help save other children even though she hadn't been able to save her sister. Curtis, she still has nightmares of that awful time."

"I don't get it." He continued to stare at Damon. "How did she connect you with the fire?"

Damon felt his face twist. "We went to a chapel in the inner city, part of the Shepherd of Love Sanctuary ministry there. I sat on her right. Sunlight streamed through a vivid stained glass window. Nancy saw me in the bright glow, the same way she saw the arsonist against the flickering flames twenty years ago."

"What did she do?" Curtis sat like someone frozen in time.

"Ran out. It took weeks and working together to save a little boy from fear and a permanently crooked leg before she would tell me why. Tonight I got the whole story."

"And you wouldn't lie about it, even to keep her." Curtis shook his head in disbelief. "Doesn't it get tiresome, being Saint Damon?"

"You'd better be thanking whatever gods you believe in I have a code of honor or you'd be picking yourself up off the hall floor," Damon told him. "Now, are you going to release me from my promise?"

"What's in it for me?" An avaricious gleam came into the dark, watching eyes. "I might just do that, if the price is high enough to make it worth it."

Damon felt the blood drain from his face. He shook his head to clear the anger, disillusionment, final hope for Curtis from his thoughts.

"I think you'd better go. But before you do, listen to

me and listen hard. Don't come back. Ever. From the time you could toddle, you've been in trouble. How does it feel to have broken the hearts of everyone who ever cared about you? I'm through, Curtis. I hope I never see you again as long as I live. Oh, I'll continue to pray that someday God will snap you up short and make you realize what you are." His voice rang in the silent apartment. "Until that happens, I have no brother."

"And you're supposed to be such a great Christian." Red-hot fury filled Curtis' eyes. "I'll get out, all right, but don't count on my turning into a Bible-thumping, hymn-singing hypocrite like you. I don't claim to be anything, but I wouldn't throw you out. Remember that. I'm a better man than you are, Dr. Barton. I always have been and I always will be."

He rose, crossed the room, and went out. The door closed behind him with a solid thud that spelled finality. Damon had never felt worse in his life. His brother's accusations stood in solid formation to arraign him, grotesque, accusing. In spite of everything Curtis was or was not, he had spoken the truth. No matter the extent of Damon's transgressions, the strange loyalty that kept his brother crawling back—and Damon realized it was loyalty, not just the need for a safe place—went so deep Curtis would never give up on him.

"God, what have I done?" He stumbled to the couch where Curtis had sat indicting him. "How often have you told us to forgive? Seventy times seven. How often have you forgiven me? Ten times that number? A hundred?" He remembered the time he had spent in juvenile detention center, hating every minute of it, feeling the injustice. He thought of how evil influences had brought pressure to him; how the young boy he once was had been miraculously delivered by a warden who believed in him—he held out the hope of parole when Damon would have sunk to the level of others who had been there before. He remembered the day of his release. His tortured spirit had gradually opened folded wings, and he had seen how terrible choices could be. Had God's Holy Spirit spoken to his troubled heart at that moment? He never knew. He simply knew that a succession of people came into his life, each at the right time, all with the words of life that had resulted in Damon's accepting the servanthood of God.

Slowly other thoughts intruded on his suffering. He must inform the hospital Nancy wouldn't be there for a time. He dialed, gave the information. Unlike with the Caxtons, Damon held little back from his director friend. Next he contacted Dr. Cranston and arranged time off. Robert knew the situation up until tonight and instantly agreed.

"Keep trusting in that God of ours," Dr. Cranston advised. "I'll be praying."

A quick call to Nancy completed his preparations. Damon walked to the window, looked into the dark streets, and shuddered. Could the Lord have felt this way when He set forth in search of lost sheep in the scriptures? Both Matthew and Luke had recorded the matchless parable of God's love for His children. Neither had given the details of the search but Damon remembered the beloved hymn often sung in church, "The Ninety and Nine."

He'd always had to take a deep breath as the graphic

interpretation told of the rough, steep road that tore the Shepherd's feet; the deep waters; the darkness and desert and mountains. Now his heart swelled within him at the final, glorious moment when the Shepherd hoisted his lost sheep on his shoulders and rejoiced. Determination slashed through him. In quick strides, Damon hastened across the living room, into the bedroom, and exchanged his lounging coat for dark slacks, a dark sweater. *Dark clothing for dark deeds*, he thought—and rejected the idea. He tried to become Curtis and decide what he would do. Turned from his brother's door, would he flee and be swallowed up in the shadows? Seek out companionship, no matter how unsavory? Mind sterile as instruments from the autoclave, he snatched a warm jacket then knelt by his bed.

"I don't know where he is. You do." After long moments, he rose and began his search for the brother who had set his feet on the wrong path long ago. For three days and nights Damon searched. Neither his desire to contact Nancy nor his duties on hold deterred him. He talked with bag ladies, pushcart people, those at Shepherd of Love Sanctuary and Clinic. The earth might as well have opened and swallowed Curtis for all the trace he found. No one had seen him. No one followed Damon, either, although his car boldly sat in its usual spot during his visits to shower and change and he took no special pains to hide it while visiting the inner city. The fourth night he dragged home. Either a lot of people were ignorant, lying, or didn't care. Damon hadn't dug up a single clue to his brother's whereabouts. Time and again he had put Curtis in God's hands, only to feel he himself must be doing something. The clock struck nine as he opened the door and stepped inside. Right on cue, the phone rang. "Let the answering machine get it," he muttered. He'd left his pager home during his search and, with one or two exceptions, failed to return calls on the machine. Some inner sense rebuked him. Damon sighed and wearily lifted the receiver.

"Dr. Barton."

"Damon?" Paul Hamilton sounded far away. "Come over to Shepherd of Love, Surgery, if you will. Okay?"

A chill swept through him. "Of course, but why?" He felt the answer before it came.

"We have a badly beaten patient here who needs some of my best work. He won't let me go ahead until you come." Paul paused and Damon's world rocked. "He says he's your brother."

"I'm on my way." Damon put the phone down, ran out, and set a new record for fast but careful driving to the hospital. He burst into the emergency ward but slowed to a rapid walk. His long training in not alarming other patients and their families took over.

"Curtis Barton?"

"He's gone up to Surgery. Dr. Hamilton will meet you there. He wants to talk with you before you see the—your brother." Compassion rested in the nurse's face. Damon saw the same look in Lindsey Best's eyes when he reached Surgery. The competent, vivacious, red-headed nurse led him to where Paul Hamilton stood scrubbing, then began her own preparations.

"Want to be in on this?" Paul shot at him.

"Yes." Damon stripped off his jacket. "What happened?"

"Disturbance not far from here, four guys beating your brother. People standing there gawking or running back in shops. Some college girl evidently couldn't take it. She sure has guts. She ran out toward the middle of the street screaming at the gang members. Her courage galvanized others into action—a girlfriend who works at a small restaurant hollered at her and at the owner. He called the police. They got there stat. The college girl identified them; they're in the slammer. It won't surprise me if they turn out to be members of a gang the cops have been after for a long time." He turned his level gaze on Damon and held up his sterilized hands for gloves. "I'm not asking and I don't want to know what your brother's connection with them is. The police will. Right now, we've got a job to do. If you think there's a problem since you're related, say so. Otherwise, just be there."

"No problem, and I will." Damon signaled to a nurse for sterile gloves. "How bad is he?"

"Contusions, deep gashes on arms—he threw them up to protect his face—on legs. One knife wound in the abdomen. Doesn't appear to have struck the vitals. I wanted to go ahead but he said not until you came. The guy's got grit." A reluctant admiration shone through his grimness.

"Yes." Damon pushed through into the Operating Theatre. "I'm here, Curtis."

"End of the line?" His gaze demanded the truth.

"Sure hope not. They got the gang."

"I saw. Gutsy girl yelled." His eyelids twitched. "Been thinking. . .what you said."

"Let's get you patched up," Damon crisply ordered. "Plenty of time to talk later. The rest of our lives." Something cried out inside him that if the knife wound had gone too deep, Curtis might not have much life left.

"Another chance?" Suddenly the pallid figure changed to the wayward older brother Damon had adored, always in trouble, always pleading for another chance.

"Of course. We're brothers, aren't we?"

The surgical staff took their places. The anesthesiologist stepped forward, hesitated when Curtis slowly shook his head. "Tell the truth, Damon." One drop escaped when he closed his eyes.

Through a welter of feelings Damon observed the procedures, noting Paul Hamilton's skill in repairing the supine body on the table. He breathed a sigh of relief when Paul murmured, "No penetration of vitals," and later when he added, "Looks good."

After closing he stepped back, dropped his mask, and grinned at Damon. "Thanks be to God, I see no reason he won't be good as ever before long."

Dr. Barton thought of the way Curtis had looked when he said, "Tell the truth." Did he mean about his shady activities? Surely not. Curtis must have been releasing his brother from a twenty-year-old promise.

He saw Paul's puzzled look when he said, "Good as ever isn't enough. Pray that he will be better," but he didn't explain. Only time could show how the near brush with death would affect the lost sheep.

twelve

Curtis Barton sent a weak smile to Damon when he stepped into his hospital room. The other bed lay empty, waiting for the next patient. Autumn leaves blew outside the long, sparkling window, and a hint of blue sky showed through a gathering cloud mass that hinted at rain.

"Well, here I am."

How like Curtis! Damon laughed, glad for the return of his cocky brother. He remembered the days following surgery, when a stubborn infection had developed. It had taken massive doses of antibiotics to knock it in the head.

"Hey, old man, feeling better today, huh?"

"Don't call me old man." Yet affection shone in the dark eyes so in contrast with the crisp pillowcase. "Uh, Damon, did I do much mumbling? My memory's kind of hazy."

"Some." *Now what?*

"Forget what I said. Okay?" Curtis grimaced.

His brother's spirits dropped to an all-time low. Then Curtis hadn't released him from his promise after all. Damon still couldn't tell Nancy the truth. He forced a grin. "Don't worry about it." Damon glanced at his watch. "Sorry, I have to run. I'll be back in later."

"See you."

"Right."

Damon walked out, wanting to beat his fist against the wall. Just when his hopes had been raised to the highest heaven, a few words had sent them plunging to the depths of despair.

"God, won't he ever change?" Damon whispered, then firmly sent his personal problems scooting out the back door of his mind. He had work to do. Still, he knew the moment he ended his rounds and had time alone, those same worries would slip in through the cracks and torment him again. How thrilled he had been, how free, when he anticipated the happiness in Nancy's face at his story. Even though a nagging little wish she had been able to trust him without concrete proof persisted, he wrote it off as asking too much.

"I wish I had called her and told her everything the minute Curtis got out of surgery," he passionately cried out in the privacy of his room that evening. It had been impossible. Dealing with the police, sticking by Curtis while he had fought his way back to health, and allowing himself only the few hours of sleep his body demanded had given no opportunity to do more than briefly call Nancy. At least he'd had good news for her. With the gang members safely incarcerated she could return to Shepherd of Love without fear. It had turned out as Paul Hamilton predicted: The hit men were wanted on far more serious charges and unless justice failed, would receive heavy sentences for their crimes.

Deep regret filled the pacing doctor. Was it quixotic to bind himself to a childhood vow, given under duress?

The courts of the land held such vows invalid. Damon shook his head. Through all the misery of growing up the one thing he had never done was go back on his word.

"God, I didn't even know You when I promised," he prayed. "Yet until Curtis releases me, I cannot speak— even if it means losing Nancy." The thought appalled him. To find a woman who could complete his life, truly be his helpmate in their work together for the Master, then lose her? Unthinkable. The other side of the picture was loss of his own self-respect if he followed the dictates of his heart and broke his pledge of silence. Damon finally knelt, turned the whole thing over to God, and fell into bed. At least Curtis had been spared, been given time to change, if he would.

Damon watched for signs of softening in his brother each time he visited him. If they existed, they lay so deep under layers of living they couldn't be readily detected. A few times a quizzical expression came to the watching eyes and once the recuperating patient had asked, "What's with you, little brother? You act like your favorite dog died."

"Tired," Damon admitted and yawned mightily. He knew Curtis didn't believe him by the way one eyebrow shot up.

Another time his brother casually asked, "What's become of the nurse? You can't be spending much time with her, hanging around here all the time and getting in my hair."

In spite of his misery, Damon caught the rough appreciation behind the sting in the words. "No."

"Did she turn out like all the rest of them?"

"No. You should know why I'm not seeing her."
Damon turned on his heels and marched out, back stiff
as if he had a steel rod instead of a spine.

"Hey, wait a minute. . ." Damon didn't halt. Wasn't
it bad enough to be alienated from the woman he loved
without Curtis airing and dissecting it like a beginning
biology student?

The few glimpses he had of Nancy proved unsatisfy-
ing, and he again avoided her as much as possible except when their work threw them together. How long
could things go on this way, he wondered. His lips set in
a hard line. Only God could straighten things out and it
didn't look like He was in any hurry.

&

"How long will we go on like this, God?" Nancy
Galbraith wearily dropped to the sofa in her pleasant
living room after a taxing day's work. Two new patients,
one of them so obstreperous it had taken more energy
than she felt she possessed to settle him down, had dis-
rupted the entire Pediatrics ward. A passing glimpse of
a stone-faced Dr. Barton in the distance hadn't helped.
Nancy's heart ached. She'd kept abreast of the hospital
scuttlebutt concerning Curtis and his progress, as much
through the expression on Damon's face as the medical
reports. Shepherd of Love's family feeling stretched to
include all who entered its doors—visiting physicians,
family members, friends. Thank God Curtis lay alive
and healing! Rumor had it he'd been exonerated of any
blame in the incident; one of the hit men had confessed
they'd been hired to do a job on Curtis for identifying
the shooter in the L.A. incident. Whatever sins Curtis

had committed since he had come to Seattle remained hidden—Nancy hoped forever, more for Damon's sake than his brother's. Seeing the knifed look in Dr. Barton's face, wounded pride, brought an ever-deepening love to Nancy.

"Why should I go on holding something he did as a child against him?" she asked the quiet room. A dozen faces rose to support her growing conclusion that Damon so little resembled the boy who set the fire that not a trace of him remained. *Timmy. Amy. Eric.* They trooped through her mind. Even if the worst were true, if his careless actions had taken life, hadn't he more than repaid it through giving life and hope and health to dozens, no, hundreds of patients? By offering peace and assurance of life eternal to others?

"I don't believe he set that fire, God." Nancy lifted her chin high. "He claims to be innocent. If I really love him do I have to have documented proof he is telling the truth?"

Her hand strayed to her worn Bible. She opened it and turned to marked verses that had helped her in the past. Reading them aloud sent them deeper into her heart than ever.

"'There is no fear in love; but perfect love casteth out fear.' (1 John 4:18)

"'Faith is the substance of things hoped for, the evidence of things not seen.' (Hebrews 11:1)

"'Jesus saith unto him, Thomas, because thou hast seen me, thou hast believed: blessed are they that have not seen, and yet have believed.'" (John 20:29)

Nancy closed her Bible. *Blessed. . .have not seen*

. . .yet believed. Her eyes brimmed. She stood, went into the bedroom and reached for the phone. Her heart pounded until her ears rang along with the phone. Damon's answering machine came on. She shook her head and cradled the phone. A lifeless instrument could not convey the well of faith in Damon she realized filled her, a bottomless, flowing sea of trust. She bowed her head, heart overflowing until words would not come. Then she walked to her desk, found paper and pen, dated the page, and began to write. One page, two, drifted to the floor but her pen raced on. At the bottom of the third page she stopped, then with swift determination signed it, *All my love, Nancy,* even while rich blood pumped into her cheeks. Her high mood persisted. She addressed and stamped an envelope, put her letter inside, and sealed it. If she went back and reread what she had written, she might not have the courage to send it.

With a sense of freedom she hadn't experienced since that terrible sunlit moment in the chapel, Nancy rapidly walked the long hall, crossed the staff residence living room, and posted her letter in the box outside. It would be picked up early and Damon should receive it by late afternoon or early the next day. That night Nancy slept soundly and without nightmares. She awakened to a sense of urgency, stretched, and thanked God for the new day. With an impish smile she showered and slipped into a soft yellow uniform, then fixed herself a substantial breakfast. The next time she saw Dr. Damon Barton, she wanted it to be after he had read her letter, not across the staff dining room, out of reach and far away.

All day she smiled at her work. Children reached out

to her and received even warmer hugs than usual. One little girl asked, "Somepin' nice hap'nin', Nurse Nancy?"

"Very nice." She beamed on the child, who cuddled closer. Just before her shift ended, a call came to Nancy. One of the other nurses took it. When Nancy came out of the linen closet with a fresh pillowcase to replace one stained with orange juice by an unsteady hand, her co-worker said, "Curtis Barton would like you to stop by when you're through here."

"Curtis Barton!" Nancy froze. She hadn't seen him since that unpleasant night in the apartment.

The nurse didn't seem to notice her agitation and went to answer a call light. Nancy automatically finished her duties, ran a comb through her hair, repinned her cap, and made sure her uniform had stayed reasonably clean. Head high, with questions knocking at her mind's door, she left Pediatrics and made her way to Curtis' room.

The door stood open so she tapped on it and stepped inside.

"Nurse Galbraith?"

Could this thin-faced man be the sneering creature who had made her feel unclean? Nancy gasped and clutched at her slipping reins of poise. "You wanted to see me?"

"Yes." His eyes brightened. "Sit here, please, but close the door first."

She hesitated, wondering what he might be up to.

"You don't have to be afraid." His gaze, so like yet unlike Damon's, softened and she did as he asked.

His first question unnerved her. "Are you in love with my brother?"

"I don't see it's any of your concern," she icily told him

to overcome the riotous *yes, yes, yes* bubbling inside her.

"You are more wrong than you imagine." Curtis regained some of his spirit. "He's convinced you are the moon and stars and sun all rolled into one. Still, he's going around with his chin on the ground. You're a Christian, aren't you?"

"I am." Where this strange conversation was headed, she couldn't guess.

"You believe in forgiveness and all that?" His sharp prod found its mark. She glanced away, remembering how long it had taken for her to reach the point of Christlike forgiveness, but warmed by the letter so close to reaching Damon.

"I do." She even smiled at him.

"Then why in the name of everything you hold sacred haven't you forgiven him now that you know the truth?" Scorn turned his words to stinging bits of ice.

Nancy stared at him. When she found her voice she faltered, "What do you mean? I haven't seen Damon since you came here except on the ward." She leaned forward, hands clenched.

"You honestly mean he hasn't told you?" Incredulity and shock widened his eyes.

"Told me what?" An inkling, a suspicion too bizarre to be real crossed her mind. Curtis drew in a deep, ragged breath.

"Nancy Galbraith, you sit there and tell me you still don't know who really set the fire that killed your mother and sister?"

Dawning consciousness blended with such a kaleidoscope of emotions Nancy reeled. "Why, you?" Her strangled whisper sounded loud in the room. "All these years—how could you do it?"

"I wanted to know how much he loved me." Naked pain twisted his face.

Nancy's rising anger shattered. "How could you doubt it?" she cried. "Hasn't he stood by you through everything?" Curtis' tough-guy façade crumpled into a million pieces, leaving a vulnerable man who held out one hand.

She shrank from him, still unable to comprehend the load Damon had carried for his brother all these years. "Will you at least listen?" Taking silence for consent, Curtis told his story in broken, jerky sentences. A mother who had doted on the older son, often had ignored the younger. One bad boy, one good. "I resented his goodness and it made me even worse," he confessed. "I got in trouble again and again. The night of the fire I'd gone out with a gang of older boys. I didn't know what they'd planned. By the time I realized the terrible thing they'd done, the fire terrified me until I ran."

"And I saw you." Again Nancy saw the boy against the flames. "I thought it was Damon. Why did they show me pictures of him, not you?"

His voice hoarsened. "No one would have believed me if I had said I hadn't been in on starting the fire. I pleaded with Damon to let them think he was me. We looked even more alike then. Damon crossed his arms and said nothing when the cops came. Mama honestly believed him guilty. The real culprits had scattered. Damon never said one word in his defense except that he had set no fire. I hid out so they wouldn't see me and perhaps get suspicious. I'd already convinced Damon it would kill Mama if she learned the truth. I'll never forget my brother standing there, thirteen years old, with a face like an angel saying, "'I vow never to tell you were there until the time you say I can.'"

Curtis threw one arm over his eyes and his muffled voice sounded hollow. "They took him away. By the time the warden got him paroled I'd moved on. I won't go into what happened. Seeing us both now pretty much tells the story." He dropped his arm and looked at Nancy with anguished eyes. "All these years, I told myself, so what? I took Damon for what I could get out of him. That's how people in the world I chose survived."

. She looked into his face, saw the realization that had come almost too late. "Why are you telling me this now?"

"For some reason, Damon's and your God spared me. It only seems square to make things right if I can."

The divine spark Nancy knew lives in even the most desperate and wicked persons struggled to burn, to become a flame of self-respect. She felt she sat witnessing a soul trying to be reborn.

"Can you forgive me?" he asked, yet she knew what he really meant was, *will Damon forgive*?

The door opened. Dr. Barton stepped inside.

"What are you doing here, Nancy?" He didn't sound shocked or disapproving, merely tired.

"I asked her to come. You big jerk, why didn't you tell her the truth after I released you from your promise?" Curtis struggled to a more upright position, face blazing.

Damon's face hardened. "If you remember, you took

it back."

"I what?" Curtis stared at the tall doctor looming above him. "When?"

"The day you started feeling better, you asked if you had done much mumbling, said your memory was hazy. I told you yes and you said to forget it."

"Of all the. . ." Curtis flopped back on his pillows. "I thought maybe I'd spilled my guts about some stuff while I was out." He looked at Damon, then at Nancy. "I guess it's not that important. I told her. Everything."

Damon stepped back as if hit. His expression changed from passive acceptance to hope.

"Nancy?" She could only nod. For the first time the love in his eyes shone unclouded by doubt or secrets. Yet even while she watched, they changed. A tiny flicker of—disappointment—crept in. The next instant it vanished but the shadow left its mark. Nancy silently prayed to understand. When Damon turned back to Curtis, she stifled the urge to wrap her arms around him. Had the revelation come too late? A flash of insight told her an even greater truth than Curtis had revealed earlier. Damon grieved over her lack of trust in the face of insurmountable evidence. She shrugged off her gloom and felt her eyes shine. Dr. Damon Barton had a precious and unique gift waiting when he received his mail.

They left the room together, the pair of dedicated persons who worked with the precision of perfectly matched gears.

"I never thought he would do it," Damon said softly. "I'm glad he did."

She peered into his face and once more caught the

inscrutable gleam. They walked on, and when they reached the chapel door, he stood aside. She walked in. He followed and closed the door.

"Nurse Nancy, is there any reason I shouldn't tell you I love you more than life itself?" He put his hands on her shoulders.

"Not now." She felt his fingers tighten, then relax. The faintest of sighs came to her ears.

With sudden resolve she said, "Damon, will you do something for me? Will you go home, read your mail, and then call me?" She thought rapidly. *What if the letter hasn't yet been delivered? It should have been,* her common sense argued. *It got picked up just after dawn.*

"I think instead I'd rather go with you," Nancy reconsidered. If the mail held no letter from her, she would tell him its contents and beg his forgiveness for not trusting him more.

&

The letter lay clean and white on the top of a stack of medical journals and junk mail. Nancy snatched it up and thrust it at him. "I'll fix lemonade while you read it." Puzzled-looking but obedient, Damon sat down on the couch. Nancy watched him from the corner of her eye while he read, knowing by the way his hand stilled that he had reached the heart of the letter. She hadn't realized how deeply her words had sunk into her soul in their writing.

. . .Jesus often said even to those who loved him most, "Oh ye of little faith." You have every right to say it to me, my darling. I should have trusted you, should have

believed in your innocence against all odds. I will spend
all our years together regretting that I did not. I realize
now you could never have set the fire, even as a young
boy. Please, forgive me. All my love, Nancy.

Damon stared at the page. Nancy held her breath
until she felt dizzy from lack of oxygen. At last he stood
and came to her. "I have nothing to forgive. I understand it was too much to ask." Yet the same hint of sadness that had rested in his eyes earlier remained.

He hasn't really forgiven, Nancy knew. She clutched
the back of a chair, using it as a barricade. Unless he
did, how could they base their love on a strong founda-
tion? Hot tears scalded behind her eyes but she crowded
them back into her hurting heart.

Damon straightened as if throwing off a heavy burden. "Come out from behind that chair, Nurse Nancy. I
can't propose with you huddled there like a bird with a
broken wing. Thank God Curtis finally told the truth,
so—"

Joy began in her toes and crept upward in a surge.
"Curtis! Oh, Damon, look at the date on the letter." She
ran out of her hiding place, snatched the pages and tri-
umphantly held up page one. "Look."

His startled gaze followed her pointing finger. His
mouth dropped open.

"But—why—that's yesterday's date. You wrote this
before. . .? Oh, Nancy."

His poignant use of her name sent her to the shelter of
his arms. Her flame of faith had destroyed the last flicker
of doubt. Their love would be a steady, purified glow
and light the paths of those they served.

epilogue

Two weeks later, Nancy stood in the glow of a sun-glorified stained-glass window and became Dr. Damon Barton's bride.

They never forgot.

Coming soon to Heartsong Presents
Shepherd of Love Hospital.
Book Three: *A Kindled Spark*
by Connie Loraine

Nurse Lindsey Best and Chaplain Terence O'Shea fight dangerous, unseen forces that threaten to destroy their careers, beloved hospital, and chance for happiness.

A Letter To Our Readers

Dear Reader:

In order that we might better contribute to your reading enjoyment, we would appreciate your taking a few minutes to respond to the following questions. When completed, please return to the following:

Rebecca Germany, Editor
Heartsong Presents
P.O. Box 719
Uhrichsville, Ohio 44683

1. Did you enjoy reading *Flickering Flames*?
   ❏ Very much. I would like to see more books
      by this author!
   ❏ Moderately
      I would have enjoyed it more if _____

   _____

2. Are you a member of *Heartsong Presents*? Yes   No
   If no, where did you purchase this book? _____

   _____

3. What influenced your decision to purchase this
   book? (Check those that apply.)

   ❏ Cover   ❏ Back cover copy

   ❏ Title   ❏ Friends

   ❏ Publicity   ❏ Other _____

4. On a scale from 1 (poor) to 10 (superior), please rate the following elements.

___Heroine   ___Plot

___Hero   ___Inspirational theme

___Setting   ___Secondary characters

5. What settings would you like to see covered in *Heartsong Presents* books?

_____

_____

6. What are some inspirational themes you would like to see treated in future books?_____

_____

_____

7. Would you be interested in reading other *Heartsong Presents* titles?   ❏ Yes   ❏ No

8. Please check your age range:
❏ Under 18   ❏ 18-24   ❏ 25-34
❏ 35-45   ❏ 46-55   ❏ Over 55

9. How many hours per week do you read? _____

Name _____

Occupation _____

Address _____

City _____ State _____ Zip _____

Heartsong Presents

Settings Around the Globe!

__*Candleshine*__ by Colleen L. Reece—With the onslaught of World War II, Candleshine Thatcher dedicates her life to nursing, and then her heart to a brave Marine lieutenant. Theirs was a wartime romance, a wisp of a breeze in the sultry South Pacific, a promise made amid threats of invasion and attack. HP07

__*Drums of Shelomoh*__ by Yvonne Lehman—As a nurse, Crystal Janis has seen it all. That is, until her visit to a mission outpost in Rhodesia, Africa. A much-needed vacation becomes a series of challenging crises and a chance for lasting love. HP37

__*Search for Tomorrow*__ by Mary Hawkins—Broken in body and in spirit but hoping nonetheless for a new beginning, Abigail Brandon accepts a job as a housekeeper for the Stevens family on their farm outside Brisbane, Australia. HP42

__*River of Peace*__ by Janelle Burnham—The year is 1930. Ida Thomas has taken the job of schoolteacher in the remote village of Dawson Creek, British Columbia. Will she find a man she can truly love and know peace like a river? HP100

..... Presents ....

Great Inspirational Romance at a Great Price!

Heartsong Presents books are inspirational romances in contemporary and historical settings, designed to give you an enjoyable, spirit-lifting reading experience. You can choose from 120 wonderfully written titles from some of today's best authors like Colleen L. Reece, Brenda Bancroft, Janelle Jamison, and many others.

When ordering quantities less than twelve, above titles are $2.95 each.

Hearts♥ng Presents
Love Stories Are Rated G!

That's for godly, gratifying, and of course, great! If you love a thrilling love story, but don't appreciate the sordidness of popular paperback romances, **Heartsong Presents** is for you. In fact, **Heartsong Presents** is the *only inspirational romance book club*, the only one featuring love stories where Christian faith is the primary ingredient in a marriage relationship.

Sign up today to receive your first set of four, never before published Christian romances. Send no money now; you will receive a bill with the first shipment. You may cancel at any time without obligation, and if you aren't completely satisfied with any selection, you may return the books for an immediate refund!

Imagine. . .four new romances every month—two historical, two contemporary—with men and women like you who long to meet the one God has chosen as the love of their lives. . .all for the low price of $9.97 postpaid.

To join, simply complete the coupon below and mail to the address provided. **Heartsong Presents** romances are rated G for another reason: They'll arrive *Godspeed!*